"I'm asking you to marry me, Mollie,"

he began. He continued to speak in that deep voice of his, but Mollie heard no more after those first few words.

Deke was asking her to marry him? Deke? Asking her? For a moment she was convinced the room had started to sway before she realized that his words had put her into shock. She stared at him, only then realizing that he was still talking and she hadn't heard another thing he'd said.

"I'm sorry," she managed to blurt out. "I'm sorry, but I wasn't keeping up with what you were saying. Did I hear you correctly? Did you just ask me to marry you?"

Now it was Deke's turn to look taken aback. He frowned, as though his carefully rehearsed words had suddenly deserted him.

"Yeah," he drawled, grabbing his cup and draining it before adding, "that's what I'm trying to say here."

Dear Reader,

Spring is on the way—and love is blooming in Silhouette Romance this month. To keep his little girl, FABULOUS FATHER Jace McCall needs a pretend bride—fast. Luckily he "proposes" to a woman who doesn't have to pretend to love him in Sandra Steffen's *A Father For Always*.

Favorite author Annette Broadrick continues her bestselling DAUGHTERS OF TEXAS miniseries with *Instant Mommy*, this month's BUNDLES OF JOY selection. Widowed dad Deke Crandall was an expert at raising cattle, but a greenhorn at raising his baby daughter. So when he asked Mollie O'Brien for her help, the marriage-shy rancher had no idea he'd soon be asking for her hand!

In *Wanted: Wife* by Stella Bagwell, handsome Lucas Lowrimore is all set to say "I do," but his number one candidate for a bride has very cold feet. Can he convince reluctant Jenny Prescott to walk those cold feet down the aisle?

Carla Cassidy starts off her new miniseries THE BAKER BROOD with *Deputy Daddy*. Carolyn Baker has to save her infant godchildren from their bachelor guardian, Beau Randolph. After all, what could he know about babies? But then she experienced some of his tender loving care....

And don't miss our other two wonderful books— *Almost Married* by Carol Grace and *The Groom Wore Blue Suede Shoes* by debut author Jessica Travis.

Happy Reading!

Melissa Senate,
Senior Editor

Please address questions and book requests to:
Silhouette Reader Service
U.S.: 3010 Walden Ave., P.O. Box 1325, Buffalo, NY 14269
Canadian: P.O. Box 609, Fort Erie, Ont. L2A 5X3

Annette Broadrick

INSTANT MOMMY

Published by Silhouette Books

America's Publisher of Contemporary Romance

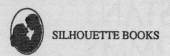

SILHOUETTE BOOKS

ISBN 0-373-19139-1

INSTANT MOMMY

ANNETTE BROADRICK

believes in romance and the magic of life. Since 1984, when her first book was published, Annette has shared her view of life and love with readers all over the world. In addition to being nominated by *Romantic Times* as one of the Best New Authors of that year, she has also won the *Romantic Times* Reviewers' Choice Award for Best in its Series for *Heat of the Night, Mystery Lover* and *Irresistible;* the *Romantic Times* WISH award for her heroes in *Strange Enchantment, Marriage Texas Style!* and *Impromptu Bride;* and *Romantic Times* Lifetime Achievement Awards for Series Romance and Series Romantic Fantasy.

Bundles of Joy

Dear Reader,

There's something very special about infants. I believe it's their innocence of life and all that awaits them. Their needs are simple. Even at that stage in life, one of our greatest needs is love.

We never outgrow our need for love and acceptance.

I am pleased to be a part of the BUNDLES OF JOY series. I've enjoyed exploring those early days of babyhood and remembering back to the times in my life when I was welcoming each of my four sons into the world.

The creation of a new life is a truly magical experience.

Annette Broadrick

Chapter One

"Well, land's sake, if it isn't Mollie O'Brien! My, but it's good to see you again, Mollie. When did you get home from college, my dear?"

At the sound of her name, Mollie paused on the steps of the Agua Verde post office and glanced around. A late spring breeze dancing across the courtyard square caressed her face, providing a touch of relief from the heat of the Texas sun.

"Oh, hi, Mrs. Krueger," she replied, when she saw the woman who had called to her. Lydia Krueger had taught Mollie's eighth-grade Sunday school class. "I came home yesterday for Maribeth's graduation. We have finals next week, then I'll be home for the summer. How are things with you?"

"Can't complain, dear, can't complain. I imagine Megan will be pleased to have you home for the summer. She could probably use some help with that new baby of hers. How old is he now?"

Mollie grinned, always eager to discuss her tiny nephew. "Danny's seven months old and such a cutie. I've really missed not being around him more this past school year. Babies seem to grow up so fast."

"Not only babies," Mrs. Krueger replied with a smile. "Why, it doesn't seem possible that you O'Brien girls have gotten so big. It seems only yesterday that Megan was fighting to keep the three of you together as a family... and you and Maribeth were still in grade school. Now here she is a new mama and both you girls are college age. I swear the time just gets away from me."

"I know what you mean. I'm four years older than Megan was when our parents died, and I'm still not sure I could handle the responsibilities Megan took on back then," Mollie admitted.

"Well, she did a fine job of it, let me tell you. Everybody can see that." Lydia Krueger glanced at her watch and shook her head as though amazed at the time. Starting toward her car, she said, "It was good to see you again, my dear. Be sure to give my regards to the family... and give that baby an extra hug for me."

"I will, Mrs. Krueger." Mollie had already turned away to enter the post office when Mrs. Krueger called to her.

"Oh, Mollie, speaking of babies, wasn't that the saddest thing about Deke Crandall?"

Mollie froze for a moment at the unexpected mention of Deke's name, before she retraced her steps to Lydia's side.

"What happened to Deke?" she managed to ask through lips that suddenly felt numb.

"Didn't Megan tell you?"

Mollie could only shake her head.

"Well, his wife, Patsy, had their baby a few weeks ago," Lydia explained, her voice losing its lilt. She paused for a moment, obviously searching her memory. "Must have been back in April. She had a little girl. I'm not real sure what happened after that. I understand Patsy started running some kind of fever and the doctors couldn't seem to do anything to help." Once again she paused, shaking her head. "I believe the baby was maybe three days old when Patsy died."

"Oh my God!" Mollie whispered, shock racing through her. "How horrible. Deke must be devastated."

Lydia nodded vigorously. "Oh my, yes. It's really just the saddest thing that's happened around here in years. The whole county turned out for the funeral, of course. It was enough to break your heart. Deke just sat staring at her lying there in that coffin. It was like he didn't know anybody else was around. People tried to talk to him, but he didn't seem to hear them. He just sat there...looking at her. He never broke down... leastways, not in front of anybody." She sighed. "I don't know what's going to happen to him and that poor little baby."

"What do you mean?"

"Since the funeral he's locked himself away in his room and won't come out. I know he must be sufferin' and all, but he's got a daughter now that needs to be cared for. We've all been real worried about them."

"Who's taking care of the baby?"

Lydia paused, blinking the moisture from her eyes. "You remember the Schultzes live out there near the Crandall place? Well, Cynthia Schultz set up a rotating schedule with her women's group from the church. Each of them takes turns staying a day and a night at a time to care for the baby. They also prepare food for Deke...not that he seems to eat much of anything these days," she added with resignation. "I don't know how long they're going to have to do that. At first, they thought they'd just help for a week or two until Deke got his head back on straight and decided to hire somebody to look after that sweet baby." Her eyes filled once again and she resolutely touched a handkerchief to them. "At this rate, the little darlin' will be walkin' before she even knows who her daddy is."

Mollie felt stunned. Even when Lydia said no more, Mollie could only stand there in shocked silence, staring at her.

Lydia patted her arm. "I really do need to go, dear. Time just seems to fritter away on me. It's good to see you back home, Mollie. Once you're settled in, why don't you come over for a visit? I'd love to hear about school and all."

Mollie glanced at her watch. "Thank you, Mrs. Krueger. I'd like that. I'll call you one of these days," she offered absently before she turned and went into the post office, her mind replaying all that she'd just heard.

Deke Crandall grieving and in pain...Deke's daughter being shuffled between well-meaning but busy women who had their own families to look after.

"Oh, Deke, I'm so sorry," she whispered softly while she gathered the accumulation of ranching magazines, the weekly newspaper and various letters and statements addressed to Travis and Megan that had been her reason for stopping by the post office in the first place.

She continued to the grocery store and mechanically filled the list Megan's housekeeper, Mrs. Hoffmeyer, had given her earlier that morning while she continued to mull over what she had learned.

Once everything was in the car, Mollie drove out of town toward the family ranch, absently following the route she'd learned years ago...while her thoughts replayed the first time she ever saw Deke Crandall.

The day was clearly marked in her mind. She'd been seven years old. It was so memorable because it was one of the few times in her life when she'd spent a whole day alone with her father. Normally he spent his time working on the ranch while her mother looked after the girls. She couldn't remember now where Megan had been, but she did recall that Maribeth had been running a fever and her dad had suggested to her mom that Mollie go with him while he ran a few errands.

Thrilled by the opportunity to spend time alone with her dad, she had accompanied him to town, happily tagging along while he stopped at the hardware store, the bank and stopped to have coffee with some of the ranchers at the little shop on the courthouse square.

Later they'd driven out to the Crandall ranch. As soon as they'd stepped up on the porch, she'd spotted a mama cat and her kittens. Delighted with her discovery she'd gone over to play with them while her dad had gone inside the house.

When the shouting and laughter broke out down by the barn, her natural curiosity had caused her to follow the sound around the side of the house where she had a clear view of the barn and several pens. A group of men were gathered outside one of the pens, hanging on to the railings while they cheered and called out advice to someone she couldn't see.

She'd immediately drawn closer, slipping silently among the roisterous men and peeking between the slats of the railed fence.

A man was riding a horse that was doing everything possible to throw him off. It was just like a rodeo she'd once seen, only now she was much closer to the action. She could almost taste the dust flying in the air.

She studied the man on the bucking horse. He seemed to be enjoying himself immensely, gracefully balanced high on the back of the spinning, gyrating animal. The men watching continued to yell out suggestions, laughingly predicting an unplanned departure from the saddle.

Sunlight glinted off his blond hair. She was mesmerized by the sight.

Eventually the horse slowed, then after a half-hearted stiff-legged jump and a defiant toss of his head, he stopped, his sides heaving. Two of the men vaulted over the fence and ran to the horse, steadying him while the rider climbed off, dusted his pants and walked toward the fence near where she peeked through.

Nobody had paid any attention to her presence. She continued to watch as the man came closer, opening a nearby gate that she hadn't noticed and joining the other men.

Seen up close he was as big as her daddy, his face sun-darkened, his loose-limbed stride like so many men who spent much of their time on horseback.

Then she heard her father calling her name. The blond man looked around in surprise and saw her watching him.

"Well, look here, would you? Where in the world did you come from, honey?" he asked, closing the distance between them.

She dipped her head toward her father's truck.

"What's your name?" he asked

"Mollie."

"Mollie? That's a nice name." Gravely he removed his leather gloves and extended his hand. "Pleased to meet ya, Mollie. I'm Deke."

She had to look a long way up to see his face. He must have realized how intimidating he seemed to someone her size because he immediately knelt, balancing on his heels so that they were eye level. Timidly she touched his hand, feeling the rough calluses on his palm.

"Do you live here?" she found the courage to ask.

"Sure do. At least during the summertime when I'm not in school."

She stared at him in surprise. "You still go to school?"

He threw his head back and laughed, his white teeth flashing in strong contrast to his deeply tanned face. "Yeah, I'm afraid so. I've still got another year to go. Are you in school?"

She nodded.

"How old are you?"

"Seven. How old are you?"

"Almost twenty-two."

She gathered up her courage and said, "You sure do ride a horse good."

"Why, thank you, Mollie. I'm glad you think so."

It was then that her father walked up.

"Mollie, you 'bout scared me half to death, girl. I left you playing on the porch and the next thing I knew you'd disappeared. Your mama would have my hide if I let something happen to you while I'm supposed to be looking after you."

Deke stood and faced her father. "She's okay, Mr. O'Brien. We wouldn't have let anything happen to her."

The two men began to chat and Mollie was able to study Deke to her heart's content. Up close that way she could see that his eyes were a startling green, glittering like jewels. He was as tall as her father, with broad shoulders and lean hips.

He wasn't really handsome or anything, not like men in the movies or on television, but it didn't matter to Mollie. He had spoken to her as if she was his equal. He had shaken hands with her and talked with her. All the other men had gone about their business without paying much notice to her, but he'd taken the time to draw her out.

She had never forgotten that meeting.

Somehow in her child's mind Deke had become more than just another rancher who lived in the county. She had begun to see him as an imaginary part of her life. When she was alone she got into the habit of pretending that he was there, and she would talk to him, tell him about school and about her life.

At the age of seven it was easy to imagine that once she grew up she would be old enough to marry Deke and live happily ever after.

By the age of ten, life's harsher realities intruded into her imaginary, little-girl world. Her parents were killed. Megan fought hard to keep the ranch and the family intact. Mollie, who had always loved helping her mother in the kitchen and with the housework, quickly tried to do her part in the house.

The three girls had clung together in an effort to survive the horrific loss and cherished memories of her childhood hero were put away with other childish dreams.

The final end to any dreams that might include Deke occurred when she was fifteen and heard that Deke had gotten married. It was funny now, looking back to the young girl she'd been just five short years ago, at how hard she'd taken the news after so much time had passed since she'd first seen him riding that bronco.

Oh, she'd seen Deke around town over the years, but always at a distance. She'd never spoken to him again. She doubted he even remembered meeting her that long-ago day.

But the memory had lingered for Mollie, even after she'd become old enough to know that he'd already been a grown man soon out of college when she'd barely started grade school. Blond hair and green eyes had always held a special kind of fascination for her.

Not that she expected him ever to learn about her early dreams of him, or become aware of the fact that she had been foolish enough to pretend that he would wait for her to grow up before deciding to marry.

She had never known his wife. Patsy wasn't from the area and there'd been no reason for their paths to cross once she and Deke were married.

Driving home, all she could think about was how sad that Deke should lose his wife just as he was becoming a father. Her heart grieved for him. She wished there was something she could do for him, but she couldn't think of anything that others hadn't already done.

She turned into the entrance of the O'Brien spread. There had been lots of changes in the almost three years since Megan had married Travis Kane, but the name of the ranch wasn't one of them. Maybe it was because Travis's parents owned the adjoining ranch and it would be too confusing to use the Kane name on both pieces of property.

Mostly it was known as the O'Brien ranch because it had been in the O'Brien family for over a hundred years. Their ancestor, Paddy O'Brien, had won it in an all-night poker game on one of the paddleboat steamers that plied the Mississippi back in those days. According to family legend, he'd been a riverboat gambler who'd decided to accept the win as a sign from God that he was to do something different with his life, so he'd headed west to Texas, eventually married and settled down to become a rancher.

Since there were no more O'Briens to carry on the family name, only the ranch would be there to remind people of the O'Brien legacy. Travis had no problem with the idea. But then, Travis had always had a healthy sense of his own worth.

As soon as Mollie pulled up near the back door of the house, Megan stepped out onto the porch from the kitchen and hurried to help her bring in the sacks of groceries.

"I still can't get used to finding you in the house," Mollie said to her, grinning. "Even Travis couldn't keep you inside. And yet, all Danny has to do is whimper and you're right by his side."

Megan had allowed her blond hair to grow long enough so that she now wore it pulled high in a ponytail. She shoved her bangs out of her eyes and took two of the bags while Mollie brought the last two. "Just because I was in the habit of working long, hard days doesn't mean I necessarily prefer them. I'm enjoying my time with Danny," she said, rapidly putting away the groceries. "Of course, I enjoy it a lot more when he isn't teething, but I guess that's part of the process."

"Speaking of Danny," Mollie said, "it's awfully quiet in here. What did you do to him?"

Megan laughed. "I didn't do anything. Mrs. Hoffmeyer used one of her tried-and-true remedies to help babies when they're cutting teeth. Whatever it is, it must have worked. She rubbed it on Danny's little swollen gums and within minutes he'd quietened. He was exhausted, poor baby. Ain't silence grand?" she teased.

After they'd put away the groceries, Mollie retrieved the ever-present pitcher of iced tea from the refrigerator. Filling two glasses with ice cubes and tea, she handed one to Megan and they both sat down at the large, round kitchen table.

"Speaking of babies, did you hear what happened to the Crandalls?" Mollie asked.

"You mean Patsy? Wasn't that terrible? How did you hear about it?"

"I ran into Mrs. Krueger at the post office this morning. I'm surprised you didn't tell me."

Megan shrugged. "Guess it didn't cross my mind to mention it. I mean, it isn't as though we knew them, really, although I think Travis sold Deke a couple of his horses last year. We went to the funeral. It was so sad . . . Patsy was only thirty-two.''

"Mrs. Krueger said Deke was pretty broken up.''

"Yeah, he was. Travis mentioned that his folks went out to the ranch to check on Deke a few days after the service, but Sally Whitman, who was looking after the baby when they got there, said he wasn't coming out of his room for anything or anybody.''

Mollie was silent for several minutes, wishing there was something she could do to ease Deke's pain. But, as Megan said, he didn't even know them. What could she say or do that could help him deal with such a blow?

"I like the way you are wearing your hair these days,'' Megan said during their companionable silence. "I've always thought your hair was so gorgeous . . . that luscious, dark chestnut color. The sun brings the red out in it.''

Mollie touched her shoulder-length hair. "It's funny how each of us looks different, yet we're sisters. You have the blond hair and the blue eyes.''

"Ugly eyes, you mean. Like a carnival kewpie doll.''

"You have beautiful eyes, very expressive.''

"What about you? Your eyes are so blue they look artificial. Mama always called them Irish eyes, with the thick dark lashes surrounding them.''

"Of course they're nothing like Travis's blue eyes, are they, Megan?'' Mollie teased.

Megan smiled. "No. His are almost purple, they're so blue. Yours are more like the sky, or a lake.''

"Then there's Maribeth," Mollie said, "with the flaming red hair and flashing golden eyes. We each have our own individual look, and yet, we're alike in other ways."

"Thank goodness we've been able to wear each other's clothes. Remember when I had to borrow a dress from you when Travis first asked me out on a date? I didn't even own one."

Mollie grinned. "I remember. I had to forbid you from wearing your boots with it!"

"Maribeth's almost as bad. She's still running around with the guys like she's forgotten she's a girl...she prefers to wear jeans, and is completely unaware of her striking looks."

"Is she still dating Bobby Metcalf?"

"Dating? I guess that's what you'd call it. They're always together, but I seldom see just the two of them going anywhere. There's usually a group headed off to the movies or a local rodeo, or some school activity."

"Does she still talk about marrying him?"

"In some vague future time. Right now they're excited because they both got accepted into A & M for this fall."

"Mrs. Krueger happened to comment today that the O'Brien girls are all grown up. We made it, thanks to you," Mollie said with a smile.

"Nonsense. We wouldn't have survived if you hadn't fed us and looked after us. It was a partnership and we each pulled our load." She eyed Mollie for a moment before saying, "Are you still irritated with me for insisting you go off to college?"

"More resigned than irritated. Just because we didn't have the money for you to go to school you seem to feel that Maribeth and I shouldn't be deprived of our education."

"C'mon and admit it. You've made lots of new friends and you're discovering there's a whole different world outside of Agua Verde County."

"True, but this is my home and I really miss being here. Let's face it, I'm just a homebody at heart." She folded her arms on the table and leaned forward. "To be honest, I'm jealous of Mrs. Hoffmeyer."

Megan blinked. "You're kidding."

"Well, maybe I am . . . a little. You've got to admit that she's got the place running so efficiently there really won't be anything for me to do when I come home for the summer."

"Except relax and enjoy yourself, for a change. That's what summer vacations are for. Maribeth never has trouble finding all kinds of things to do with her time."

"I know, but she's always been sociable, while I'm more content to stay home and putter around the house." She took a sip of her tea. "You know, I've been thinking . . ."

"About?"

"Deke Crandall."

Megan looked at her in surprise. "Why in the world would you be thinking about Deke Crandall? I mean, I know he's suffered a grievous loss but still...there's nothing anyone can do for him."

"That's just it. Maybe there is," Mollie mused.

"What are you talking about?"

"I've been toying with the idea of asking Deke if I could take care of his baby...I mean, until he could find somebody permanent."

"Do you mean actually live with him?"

"Well, yeah, I'd have to stay there to be able to look after an infant."

"Oh, Mollie, I don't think that's a very good idea."

"Why not?"

"Isn't it obvious? You living there with him, for whatever reason? It just wouldn't look right."

"Megan? When have you ever cared what people think?"

"About me? Never. About my sisters? I guard your reputations with my life."

"Well, maybe it's time to let us do our own guarding. If I don't care what people think, and if I can help Deke out, I'd like to do it."

"I doubt he'll agree to it. From what I hear he's in pretty bad shape."

"Well, then I guess I'll have to beard the lion in his den and discuss it with him."

"You're really serious about this, aren't you?"

"Yeah. I think I am. I couldn't get it out of my mind during the drive from town. Here's this little baby being cared for by strangers, practically orphaned if what I'm hearing is true about Deke's behavior."

"You'll be a stranger to her, too."

"At first, yes, but from what I understand, the women are taking turns keeping her so that the poor little thing isn't getting used to seeing one face she can depend on."

"And what's going to happen when it's time for you to return to school? I'm here to tell you that you can really get attached to them mighty fast."

Mollie shrugged. "That's almost three months away. I may not get the job. Even if I do, Deke may find someone to care for her permanently in a few weeks. I don't see any reason to borrow trouble before it gets here, do you?" She glanced at her watch. "I think I'll go over there and talk to him about it."

"Now?"

"Sure, why not?"

Megan laughed. "You've never been one to sit still since I've known you, but you've got another week of school before you're home for the summer. Why don't you wait and talk to him then?"

"Because I'm afraid I'll lose my courage if I don't do it today." She walked around the table and hugged Megan. "I'm fine, Mama Bear. You can stop worrying about me, okay?" She picked up the car keys and headed toward the door. "Wish me luck. I have a hunch I'm going to need it."

Chapter Two

The sound of women's voices going on and on finally registered on Deke's alcohol-soaked brain.

He groaned.

It must be changing-of-the-guard time again. Each day a new shift arrived, taking over his kitchen, taking over his house, yippin' and yappin' until he wanted to throw something at them.

At least they'd finally learned to leave him alone. He didn't want to see them, he didn't want to talk to them and he sure as hell didn't want to hear any of their well-meaning advice about what he needed to do.

He knew what he had to do. He was just too much of a damn coward to do it quick and clean. Instead he was trying to kill himself with alcohol.

The problem was that he'd never been much of a drinker. His system had slowly been tolerating more during the past few weeks, but he was ashamed to admit that he threw up almost as much as he drank.

Deke sat on the side of the bed and rubbed his face. He couldn't remember the last time he'd shaved ... or bathed ... or ate. He generally waited until late at night when the house was quiet to leave his bedroom and go to the kitchen. There was all kinds of food in the refrigerator. Everybody and her mother had brought food out here to him.

He didn't have much luck keeping it down, either.

He knew he couldn't keep on this way. He was being a self-absorbed, self-pitying, son of a— But what the hell. It wasn't a crime, was it, to sit down one day and decide that he was tired of fighting it? He'd never had any use for whiners. Now he'd turned into the biggest whiner of them all.

He froze at the sound of a high-pitched wail. He heard the tittering of the women somewhere in the house. They sounded like a gaggle of geese, for God's sake. The baby was suddenly quiet. Of course she'd shut up. With every woman in the county making certain that all her needs were fulfilled before she was even sure what it was she needed, she certainly had nothing to complain about.

Except for the fact that she no longer had a mother and she had a worthless excuse of a man for a father.

He stood, still unsteady from the quantity of bourbon he'd managed to consume the night before, and felt his way into the bathroom. He'd kept the drapes tightly closed over the windows for days. The only light coming in was the thin stripe between the edge of the windows and the drapes. Enough light to see where he was going. Not enough light to have to face his image in the mirror.

He made it to the bathroom without stumbling and reached into the shower to turn on the water. Maybe a shower would help to clear his head.

As soon as the water warmed, he stepped under the cascading spray, feeling it caress his battered body. He stood there for countless minutes, allowing the water to work its magic on bruises that were too deep within him to show.

By the time he turned off the spray, it was running cool, but his body had been scrubbed and his hair was now clean. He toweled off, already feeling exhausted from the unaccustomed exercise.

After draping the towel around his shoulders he returned to the bedroom, seeing the accumulation of bottles, glasses, dirty dishes and disheveled bedclothes. He was going to have to do something with the place. It was a pigsty. Worse than that. It was a—

A knock on the bedroom door interrupted his search for the proper description of the room he'd turned into his lair.

Who in the hell was stupid enough to knock on his door? Nobody had bothered him in here for weeks now. He thought they understood that—

Another knock sounded. "Mr. Crandall?"

Who was that? He didn't recognize the voice.

"Go away," he growled.

"Mr. Crandall?" was the immediate reply. "This is Mollie O'Brien. You probably don't remember who I am but I need to speak to you."

He glanced down at his bare body and almost smiled. Whoever the hell Mollie O'Brien was, he'd be willing to bet that he could shock the sweet little dear out of ten years' growth if he invited her in.

"Go away," he repeated doggedly. Deke walked over to the bed and sat down, grateful for the support. Damn, but he was weak! Now his own body was betraying him, which was a hell of a note. Couldn't depend on anything anymore. Absolutely nothing.

"Mr. Crandall. I know you're grieving. I know that this is a very bad ti—"

"You don't know what you're talking about! Now get away from that door and leave me alone."

"I'm not going to do that, Mr. Crandall. I'm going to stand here and pound on this door until you let me talk to you. This is really important or I wouldn't be so insistent."

For one almost uncontrollable moment Deke felt the urge to pick up the empty whiskey bottle beside his bed and throw it against the door. Only some slight sense of sanity reminded him that if he did, he would be subjecting himself to a carpetful of glass slivers.

He closed his eyes for a moment, trying to think around the helacious headache that pounded through his head like a giant kettledrum.

Whoever this Mollie O'Brien was, obviously she was not going to take no for an answer. His only other option was to get rid of her. The sooner the better. Her persistent knocking wasn't even in the same rhythm as the kettledrum in his head.

He stood up and grabbed at a shadowy pile of clothes, knocking them over. He felt around until he recognized the texture of his jeans. The burst of anger that her intrusion had created helped him to shakily step into the jeans and pull them up. He zipped them as he made his way to the door.

"Mr. Crandall?" she was saying just as he opened the door.

She stood there, her fist poised in midair, inches away from his bare chest. He stared at her, frowning. Did he know this woman? He didn't think so. She wasn't the forgettable kind. Eyes the color of a summer sky, surrounded with the longest, thickest lashes he'd ever seen, a complexion that looked like porcelain, and a tumbling mass of reddish-brown hair that framed her heart-shaped face.

She wore a simple, shirtwaist dress the same color as her eyes. *I wonder how long it took her to find a perfect match,* he wondered cynically.

"All right. Here I am. Now what do you want?"

Mollie took a step backward, staring at the large man filling the doorway that had been closed tightly against her an instant before. She hadn't been prepared to confront him in quite this fashion.

He stood there wearing a pair of faded jeans. Period. His blond hair tumbled over his forehead, and he had the beginning of a thick beard covering his cheeks. But it was his bloodshot eyes that silenced her into numb compassion. The man standing before her had seen hell—was, perhaps, still living there.

"Mr. Crandall," she said hesitantly, "I, uh, would like to speak to you, if I may."

"You've made that quite obvious. What I want to hear from you is why. Didn't those women—" he waved his arm toward the front of the house "—tell you I don't want to see anybody, I don't want to talk to anybody, I don't want company, I don't want consoling? What I want is to be left the hell alone!"

"Yes, they told me," she said quietly. "However, I still would like to speak to you."

"You would, would you?"

"Yes."

With a sigh he turned around and stalked back into the room. "Well, come on in, if you must. And close the door behind you."

Gingerly she stepped into the darkened room, her eyes working to adjust to the gloom before the closing of the door reduced the visibility even further.

Deke threw himself down on the rumpled bed and lay there, watching her without expression.

Mollie couldn't remember a time in her life when she'd felt so out of her depth. But she refused to turn away now. Not after she'd seen Deke's baby daughter. From the time she'd walked into the house and had seen the tiny infant greedily pulling on her bottle, Mollie knew she was in real danger of losing her heart to another Crandall.

Jolene had her dad's glittery eyes and a shock of almost white hair, which stood up from her tiny little face as though brushed into a spike. Her eyes had locked with Mollie's and she'd watched her every move. How could such a newborn baby be so alert?

Now more than ever, Mollie was determined to accomplish her mission.

Mollie finished closing the door and felt her way to a straight-back chair she'd spotted nearby. She brushed a pile of clothes off it and, once seated, clasped her hands together in her lap, straightening her spine. "I've come to apply for the position of housekeeper and to care for your daughter."

"No," he replied immediately. "Now get out."

"But, Mr. Crandall, you're going to need—"

"It's none of your concern what I'm going to need. I don't want some high school baby-sitter trying to look after—"

"Mr. Crandall, please. If you'll just give me a moment to explain. I'm twenty years old. I've just completed my second year at UT in Austin. My sister Megan had her baby last November and I've had some experience looking after him. I—"

"O'Brien...of course. You're one of the O'Brien girls. I remember now. You were just a kid when your folks were killed."

"Yes. I was ten. I grew up fast. I looked after the household until I left for college. I believe that I could help you until you're ready to begin interviewing for a full-time permanent caretaker."

"What makes you think I need someone? The baby's being cared for."

"Yes, but you can't expect these women to continue interrupting their schedules indefinitely, whereas I have nothing else to do this summer. I can give you three months in which to look for a replacement."

Deke stared at the shadowy figure of the woman seated across the room from him. She certainly hadn't been scared off by his manner and he knew he was being a complete bastard.

He knew. He just didn't care.

But something inside reminded him that a part of him had to care, for the baby's sake. It wasn't her fault that his life had turned to—

Deke sat up and swung his legs to the floor. Facing her now, he asked, "Mollie? Is that your name?"

"Yes."

"I don't guess I understand. Why would you want to tie yourself down with so much responsibility? You aren't that old, after all. Why aren't you making plans to spend the summer socializing with your friends? You're young. You're attractive. Surely you have a busy social life."

"I left my so-called social life in Austin where I'm certain it will be waiting for me when I return in the fall. In the meantime, I'm used to responsibility and there's nothing for me to do at my sister's place. She already has all the help she needs."

Deke pushed himself up and made his way barefoot into the bathroom without saying anything. He ran some water, rinsed out a glass, then filled it. He looked into the medicine cabinet until he found some over-the-counter pain medication. Tipping out three tablets, he swallowed them, then chased them down with the water.

For the first time in days he stared into the mirror in front of him. Light from the frosted glass of the bathroom window illuminated the room.

It was not a pretty picture. Black puffy circles decorated his eyes, making him look like some damn raccoon. He was well on his way to having a full-fledged beard when he'd been clean shaven all his life.

Let's face it, Crandall, he thought to himself. *You're messed up. Really messed up. Here's a chance to get back on track. Are you going to blow this off, too?*

He took his time before returning to the other room. He was giving her a chance to leave. When he walked back into the bedroom he saw that she hadn't moved.

"Do you know how to make coffee?"

"Yes."

"How about putting on a pot of coffee while I shave? After that we'll talk in my office, away from all those women."

At least he was willing to talk to her. Without saying anything more, Mollie left Deke's room, quietly closing the door behind her.

She walked to the kitchen and immediately had everyone's attention.

"We tried to tell you, honey. Don't take anything he said personal. He's just hurtin' and—"

"He asked me to make him some coffee," Mollie said, walking over to the cabinets and searching for the necessary ingredients.

The women exchanged a look. "He did?" one of them asked in surprise.

"Uh-huh." She quickly found what she needed and started the coffeepot.

"Well, I wouldn't have believed it," another one muttered.

"Of course you know, Mollie, that you can't possibly stay out here all by yourself like that. It's real sweet of you to offer to help him and all, but it just wouldn't look right for you to stay out here."

"Why is that, Mrs. Ferguson?" she asked, leaning against the cabinet and facing the three women sitting at the table.

"Well, it's obvious, of course. I mean here you are a good-looking single girl and then there's Deke in there..." She allowed her voice to drift off.

"Who has just lost his wife," Mollie added, "and who is in complete despair. Somehow I don't think he's going to be in the least interested in who's keeping Jolene."

"That's the truth," one of them muttered.

"Anyway, he hasn't said he'd hire me. But I will talk to him about it." She filled a large mug with black coffee and walked into the hallway. She spotted his office off the long living room and went inside.

She wondered if he would really come out of his room or whether he'd just decided to say whatever was necessary to get rid of her. She placed the cup of coffee on the desk and wandered over to the window.

From there she had a panorama of the rolling Texas hills that were part of the Crandall ranch. Closer, she saw the large barn and holding pens surrounding it where she'd seen a much younger, happier Deke for the first time.

He'd changed in many ways. His broad shoulders were heavier, more muscled. Or maybe it was just the fact that she'd now seen him without a shirt for the first time. Seeing him again after all these years had been a real jolt to her system.

She was no longer seven years old, but he still had a strong effect on her.

Maybe everybody—Megan, Mrs. Ferguson, Deke— was right. Maybe she had no business trying to care for Jolene or Deke. She was already too emotionally involved. It didn't matter that he hadn't known who she was. It didn't matter that he had no idea how he had become an imaginary childhood friend to her while she was growing up.

She smiled at the memory of the many nights when she'd lain in bed and talked to him, just as though he were there in the room with her. She would tell him about her day, the good things and the not so good things. He would always listen, applauding her when she had a triumph, consoling her when she'd been hurt in some way.

Now that she'd been confronted with the real man, Mollie had to face how much she'd idealized him over the years. In person, he was much bigger, much more male, and certainly not the image conjured up by an innocent child's need for a companion.

The sound of the door closing behind her caused Mollie to turn around.

He'd shaved and dressed. He walked over to the desk in that long-legged stride of his that she remembered, then sank into the chair behind the desk. He picked up the cup with both hands and brought it to his mouth.

Mollie slowly walked over to the two chairs arranged in front of his desk and sat down in one of them.

He didn't look at her. Instead he concentrated his attention on the contents of the cup. It was only after he'd drained it that he spoke, and that was merely to ask, "Is there any more coffee?"

She gave him a long look before she quietly said, "Of course. There's a whole pot . . . in the kitchen."

He flinched at her words. She couldn't believe it. This large specimen of manhood actually appeared intimidated by the prospect of going into the other room to get more coffee.

She took pity on him. "Would you like for me to get you some more?"

His bloodshot gaze looked at her as though she had offered him untold riches. "Please," he murmured fervently.

She took his cup and left the room.

Only one of the women remained in the kitchen and she was in the process of changing the baby. "I'm going to put Jolene in her room for a nap," the woman said.

"The others have gone?"

"Oh, yes. They've got to get home to their families."

Mollie poured the coffee, then on impulse picked up the carafe and took it back into the other room with her. When she walked inside, she saw that Deke was resting his head against the back of his leather chair, his eyes closed.

The harsh light coming in from the window was cruel to his features. His eyes were sunken and surrounded with dark circles, while deep lines scored his face on either side of his grim mouth.

She set the cup and carafe on the felt pad in front of him and silently reseated herself.

He opened his eyes and stared blankly at her. Slowly his gaze focused and sharpened. He reached for his cup and took a long swallow. "You make a mean cup of coffee, I'll give you that... but you're too young," he finally said.

"For what?"

Her calm rejoinder seemed to catch him off guard, for his cheeks grew ruddy with color. "To be anybody's nurse or housekeeper," he muttered. "You're too damn young."

"All right," she replied agreeably. "Maybe I am. But you need somebody and I'm the only one volunteering at the moment. You need some help. There's nothing wrong in admitting it. Who's looking after your ranch?"

He glanced over at the window. "I have a foreman."

"When's the last time you spoke with him?"

"What's it to you?"

"Nothing. I'm just wondering how long you're going to keep hiding in that room, pretending that—"

"I'm not pretending anything, damn it! I know what's happened. I know I can't change anything. I know..." His voice drifted into silence.

"You can change a few things, Mr. Crandall. You can change what you're doing today. You can come out of that room and start showing some interest in your daughter and in your ranch. You can—"

"Who the hell do you think you are, that you feel you can sit and preach to me? You don't know anything about what I'm going through...what it's like to—" He suddenly caught himself, realizing what he was saying and who he was saying it to. "Sorry," he mumbled. "I forgot about your folks."

"All I'm saying is that you have a good reason, a very good reason, to keep going. You've got a daughter who needs you. And you need her, even if you don't think so at the moment."

They sat in silence and stared at each other for a long while before Deke gave a deep sigh and finally spoke. "I can't deny what you're saying, but I just can't deal with all of this right now.''

He got up and walked out of the room. Mollie continued to sit there as she heard his booted footsteps echo down the hallway. The bedroom door slammed, causing Jolene to give a brief *"wahh"* of surprise from her room. Mollie could hear the woman with her murmur something in a soothing voice. The baby made no more protest and the house was silent.

After several moments, Mollie eventually stood and slowly left the room. She walked through the empty kitchen and let herself out of the house. Once she reached her car, she stood and looked around at the cluster of buildings.

What a shame, she thought. If he could only understand how much he still had to be thankful for. Well, at least she had tried.

Mollie drove away from the Crandall ranch, her heart heavy. Perhaps she could think of something more she might be able to do to help, but at the moment her mind was blank.

Deke was in bad shape. She wished it didn't hurt so much to see him that way. There was no rhyme or reason for her to have such a strong reaction to a man she really didn't know. She had no explanation for it. She just knew that she hurt for him, and she'd had to walk away.

Chapter Three

"I wish he weren't so stubborn," Mollie said that night over dinner.

"The man's got to be hurtin', Mollie," Travis said in his deep voice.

"Of course he is, but that doesn't mean he has to shut himself away and stop living."

"I'm just relieved he turned you down," Megan said. "That's way too much responsibility for a young girl like you to take on."

"I can't believe I'm hearing you say that, Megan," Mollie replied. "You were four years younger than me when you took on the responsibility of this entire ranch and Maribeth and me, besides."

"Which certainly qualifies me to be able to voice an opinion in the matter," Megan immediately retorted.

"Don't you see, honey? I don't want you to have to give up so much of your youth when you don't have to. I had to do what I did if I was going to hang on to the ranch for all of us as well as keep the family together. It was worth it to me."

Mollie looked down at her empty plate. "Maybe this is worth it to me," she said quietly.

After a charged silence, Travis said, "I'm not certain that I understand why, Mollie. I didn't even know you knew Deke."

She shrugged. "I don't. I mean, I knew who he was, but that's all. I just keep thinking about that baby, needing someone in her life."

"But it isn't your problem, honey, as long as Deke's neighbors are helping out."

"I suppose," she said, knowing her reluctance to the idea of giving up on Deke made no sense, not even to her. She was an adult now, too old to confuse her childhood imaginary friend with the man of the same name.

"Good," Megan said, pushing away from the table. "Who's ready for some pie and coffee?"

Mollie knew that the subject was over.

Three weeks later Mollie was playing with Danny when the phone rang. Since she was the closest, she grabbed it.

"H'lo?"

"Is Mollie there?"

She recognized the gruff voice immediately. Bouncing Danny against her hip to keep him quiet, she replied in as calm a tone as possible, "This is she." She could feel her heart racing.

"Uh—Mollie—uh, this is Deke Crandall."

"Yes, Mr. Crandall?"

She heard a noise that sounded suspiciously like a groan. "Would you mind calling me Deke? I mean, I know I'm old enough to be your father, but damn, I hate being called mister. I feel like I should be hobbling around."

She grinned. "You would have had to be a terribly precocious fourteen-year-old to have been my father... Deke."

He grunted. "I'd probably been better off than this," he muttered, as though to himself. He cleared his throat. "The thing is, all these women are driving me plumb out of my head with all their cackling and yacking. I was wondering if... Well, if maybe you'd... What I mean is, if you could just come over and help me out for the next few days." He coughed. "I kinda lost it this morning and went stompin' into the kitchen and told 'em all to get out of my house and give me some peace and quiet... so they did... and now I don't know what I'm going to do. So far the baby's still asleep but when she wakes up she's going to expect somebody to feed her and dress her and do all those things..." He waited but Mollie didn't say anything. She heard a heavy sigh. "So what I was wondering was... I mean, if you're still willing to help me out for a few days like you once mentioned...would you consider coming over here, uh, now?"

It would serve him right if she said no. His neighbors had just been trying to help him. However, she had to admit that he'd seemed to be shaken by the presence of the women the last time she'd seen him.

Of course, she really didn't have anything else to do with her time, which had really been dragging since she'd gotten home.

Besides . . . she *had* offered her services, hadn't she? Anyway, it would only be for a day or two...probably.

"Uh, hello? Mollie? Are you still there?"

The man sounded desperate. "I'm here. I was just thinking about your offer."

"Look, I'd be willing to pay you whatever you want. I know I wasn't very gracious when you were here before and I'm really sorry."

She didn't want him groveling, for heaven's sake. "I suppose I could come over and help out, if you'd like."

He didn't try to disguise his sigh of relief. "Thank God. Please come right away. I'll be watching for you."

I'll just bet you will, she said, hanging up and going to find Megan to tell her that she was leaving. She already knew her sister would be less than overjoyed with the news of her latest employment opportunity.

Deke stepped out onto the porch as soon as she hopped out of the car. He looked as bad, if not worse, than he had when she'd last seen him. That was probably the last time he'd shaved.

"Is she awake?" she asked, coming up the steps to where he stood.

"No."

She looked at him and shook her head. "When's the last time you ate?"

The glare he gave her was obviously meant to annihilate her. She ignored it and walked past him. "Go get cleaned up. You look like a grizzly bear. No wonder you ran the women off. They probably didn't realize you were human."

He followed her into the kitchen. "So why aren't you scared off? I've yelled at you a few times, haven't I?"

She just shook her head and started opening cabinets and cupboards. "I don't scare easy," she said, not looking around. "Don't forget to shave."

Mollie began to mix up a batch of biscuit dough, found some bacon in the deep freeze and rummaged in the refrigerator for eggs. There were several partially eaten casseroles that she guessed had been brought over by well-meaning neighbors.

Something had to be done about Deke. Enough was enough. Somebody had to get through to him and it looked as if the only person left around him was her.

When she heard him coming down the hallway some time later she asked, "How do you like your eggs?"

"Over easy." His voice sounded very muted.

She removed the bacon from the pan. "Sit down. Your breakfast is almost ready."

"Breakfast? It's almost two o'clock in the afternoon."

"So what?" She placed a heaping platter on the table, filled with steaming biscuits, hash browns and bacon. She returned to the stove to prepare his eggs.

Deke sat down and stared at the plate in front of him, wondering what he was doing sitting there looking at food when all he wanted was another glass of bourbon and permanent oblivion.

Slowly he began to eat. The biscuits were so light they almost floated off his plate. Patsy had never been able to—

No. Thinking that way lay madness. Stick to the moment. That was the only way he was going to be able to survive—moment by moment.

"Thank you," he murmured to his plate.

"For what?"

"For coming over as soon as I called. For continuing to kick my butt when I've been nothing but rude to you and everybody else."

She set a plate of perfectly prepared eggs in front of him, then sat down across the table from him. "I really do understand what you're going through, Deke. But enough's enough. Taking out your hurt and anger on everybody else isn't going to get you anywhere."

He kept returning his gaze to her in silence while he methodically continued to eat, bite by bite, until everything on his plate was gone. "Yeah," he finally said, "I guess you do understand, at that."

Deke noticed with a sense of surprise that he had eaten everything on his plate. His stomach hadn't forgiven him for his latest bout of bourbon, but it was calming. If he remained quiet for a while, perhaps his stomach wouldn't rebel against him this time.

"I didn't take time to pack anything because you sounded rather desperate, but sometime today I'm going to have to—"

"No," he immediately said. When he saw the look of surprise on her face, he said, "I mean, you can't go and leave the baby. She might wake up before you can get back here."

She smiled. "You don't have to be afraid of her. I can show you how to—"

"No! You stay here. I'll go pick up your things."

She could see that he was very serious. She thought about what he was offering to do. According to what she'd heard about him, he hadn't left the ranch since Patsy's funeral. He'd stayed locked up in his room. She didn't know what had set him off this morning, but she was glad that something had broken through his apathy. Maybe he hadn't really meant to run the women off, but at least he'd taken some action rather than staying sunk in his dispair.

She nodded. "All right. I can call Megan and have her pack a few things for me."

A sound from the other room made both of them turn toward the hallway. When Mollie glanced back at Deke, he looked panicked. "I don't know anything about babies. Nothing. If you'll go check on her I'll be on my way to get your things, okay?" Deke pushed away from the table and stood. He paused for a moment, as though he was still having a little trouble moving too fast. "I'll be back shortly."

Mollie watched him cross the ranch yard to a long low building where she could see a pickup truck. Then Jolene let out a wail, reminding Mollie of why she'd been called to the rescue.

Jolene would be the person who would help ease Deke's pain, if he would let her. Mollie hurried into the other room.

"Hello, there, little one," she said softly as soon as she reached the side of the crib. "It looks like it's just you and me, babe, for the next few days. Shall we get acquainted?"

Mollie had already seen the schedule that the women had posted on the refrigerator and knew that it was time for Jolene's next feeding. She'd already prepared a bottle, so all she needed to do at the moment was to replace the wet diapers and get acquainted with her new charge.

Jolene watched her with a solemn expression, her green gaze appearing more direct and knowing than Mollie would have expected from a tiny baby. Her hair stood in a peak over her brow. Mollie smoothed her hand over the crown of her head, pressing the tuft down, only to see it spring upright as soon as she moved her hand.

"All right, cutie, it looks like your hair is going to do exactly what it wishes. Is that a hint to your personality as well? Something tells me you're going to be as stubborn and strong-willed as your daddy. I'm lucky I won't be taking care of you for more than a few days.''

Within a few minutes Jolene was sucking determinedly on a nipple that seemed too big for her rosebud mouth. Her concentration was intense as she kept both her tiny fists and her eyes closed.

Still holding her, Mollie went to the phone and called Megan. As soon as her sister answered, she explained that Deke was on his way over to get her things.

"I doubt I'll be here more than a few days. It looks like he's ready to start rebuilding his life. I'm sure he'll start interviewing housekeepers soon."

Megan sighed. "I wish I felt better about all of this."

"Why don't you keep your mothering instincts for Danny and let me deal with this, okay?"

Megan chuckled. "Ah, to be twenty again, that wonderful age when we know everything about everything and life can be controlled and directed to suit our preferences."

"You don't have to talk as though you're in the twilight of your years, Megan," Mollie replied with a hint of irritation. "You're not even close to thirty yet."

"Oops, there goes Danny. I'll talk with you later. I may be able to get over to see you tomorrow or the next day, in case you need some help. That is…" she paused, then said in a wry voice, "if you don't think I'm trying to mother you too much."

Mollie grinned to herself. "No. That would be great. I want you to see Jolene. She's a real cutie and already looks just like Deke. Besides, I'm sure I could use some pointers on how to take care of her."

"Really? Well, it's good to know I can help you with something!"

"Oh, you! Goodbye, now," Mollie said, replacing the phone in its cradle. She gently pulled the bottle away from Jolene and placed her on her shoulder, gently rubbing her tiny back to get rid of any air bubbles she might have swallowed in her vigorous efforts at eating.

Mollie glanced around the kitchen. The women had done a good job of keeping everything clean and polished. However, she had a hunch that nobody had been in Deke's room since she was here and it had already been a complete mess then. As soon as she finished feeding Jolene, she'd attack his room before he returned with her things.

Once the baby was fed, rediapered, and put down for another snooze, Mollie went down the hallway and opened the door to Deke's bedroom. The drapes were still drawn and the air was stale.

She walked over to the windows, pulled the drapes and opened the windows wide, then turned to survey the room. It looked like the site of a natural disaster. She shook her head and gathered dirty clothes, pulled rumpled sheets from the bed, then carried the bundle she'd gathered to the laundry room.

Another trip had her gathering dirty dishes and empty bottles. She started her actual cleaning in the bathroom, surprised at how modern it looked. Deke must have had it remodeled in the past few years. Mirrors lined the walls, an oversize tub with water jets was below a large frosted glass window. A separate glass shower stall was in another corner.

The white and hunter green tiles matched the green towels and throw rugs.

As soon as she finished the bathroom, she made sure Jolene was all right and then started on the bedroom. By the time she had vacuumed, dusted, put clean sheets on the bed and found a summer bedspread to replace the heavier one that needed to be dry cleaned, the room was filled with light and fresh air.

While cleaning the bedroom she'd found a shattered glass-framed picture of Patsy lying almost under the bed. After making sure she'd gotten all the pieces of glass that had fallen into the rug, Mollie carefully removed the photograph from the frame. It had been sliced by the broken glass but she knew Deke would want the picture when he was over the worst of his grief. She would see about having it mended and reframed and would give it to him later.

She stared down at the laughing woman in the picture, wishing she'd known her better. Of course there was a large gap in their ages—Megan had said Patsy was thirty-two. She looked like she would have been fun. Her brown eyes sparkled and her smile was mischievous, as though she'd been teasing the person who had snapped the photo.

Mollie felt the sadness of what such a loss would mean to Deke and Jolene. Sometimes it was extremely hard to understand why these things had to happen.

She hoped that her presence would help him to continue to deal with his new situation. She wanted to do whatever she could, not only for Deke, but for his baby daughter as well, who was too young to understand what had happened, what it meant not to have a mother.

Mollie knew only too well what that was like.

Deke had no sooner stopped his truck in front of the O'Brien homestead than Travis Kane appeared in the doorway of his horse barn and started toward him in long strides.

Deke hadn't spoken to Travis in months. Even though they lived in the same county and each owned a ranch, their paths seldom crossed. Travis bred and raised quarter horses while Deke ran cattle and sheep on his place. At one time Travis had also built himself a reputation as one hell of a bull rider and calf roper. According to county gossip, though, Travis now devoted himself full time to the ranch. Deke appreciated his eye for good horseflesh after buying two of his horses.

Deke stepped out of the truck and waited for Travis to reach him.

"Deke. It's good to see you out and about," Travis said, holding out his hand to Deke. "We were all saddened by your loss. I want you to know that." When Deke looked away without saying anything, Travis added, "So, how's that baby girl of yours doing?"

"She's okay," Deke finally muttered gruffly. "That's why I'm here. Mollie's agreed to stay over at my place and look after her until I can hire somebody permanently for the job. She was supposed to have called Megan to get her stuff together for me."

Travis pushed his Stetson to the back of his head and scratched his temple, frowning. "Nobody mentioned anything about any of this to me."

"We just decided, kinda suddenlike."

"Who is we?"

"Me . . . Mollie."

"Have you spoken to Megan?"

Deke stiffened. "Why?" he growled. "Is she her sister's keeper?"

Travis kept his voice quiet. "You might say that. She was made her legal guardian a few years back."

Deke leaned against the truck, crossing his arms across his chest. "The way I understand it, you don't need a legal guardian when you're twenty years old."

"Are you sure having Mollie over at your place is a good idea, Deke?"

"Hell, no. I'm not sure of anything anymore," he said, looking off toward the hills.

Travis studied the older man for a longer moment before he companionably touched his shoulder. "C'mon into the house. We'll have some coffee and talk to Megan."

Deke shook his head, wondering how the hell he'd gotten into this situation. He was at least five years older than Travis, more than that older than Megan and yet here he was docilely allowing the younger man to lead him into the house where he was no doubt going to be vigorously interviewed by Megan Kane before he could be considered as a possible temporary employer for Mollie. What's wrong with this picture? he asked himself.

All he wanted to do at the moment was to find himself a full bottle of bourbon and return to his darkened room. He wasn't ready for any of this. He should turn around right now and get the hell out of there.

Instead he followed Travis up the steps, across the wide porch and into the kitchen of his home.

"Hi, Deke," Megan said, sitting at the table and spooning food into the mouth of a baby sitting in a high chair. "Mollie said you were on your way over. Unfortunately I had to stop and feed Danny-boy here before I had a chance to do much."

"We came in for some coffee, anyway," Travis said, filling two cups with steaming black liquid. He placed them on the table and motioned for Deke to sit down. Deke chose the chair farthest from the baby, keeping his eyes averted.

As soon as he took a sip, he glanced at Megan and said, "So this is why Mollie makes such good coffee," he said with a solemn nod of approval.

"She taught me, I'm afraid," Megan replied. "Mollie's the domestic one in this family."

Travis dropped an arm around his wife's shoulders and leaned over to give her a brief kiss. "You're doing just fine, honey. Just fine."

Deke watched the interplay between the two and felt his stomach clench. This was the way couples acted when they loved each other. Had he and Patsy ever acted that way? Maybe at first, when he'd been foolish enough to believe that she'd actually loved him, and that she'd married him out of love. But he'd found out quick enough she was real good at lying. Much too good.

Travis sat down beside Megan and smiled at his son. "Looks like you're wearing as much as your eating, boy," he said.

The baby slapped his hand on the high-chair tray and gurgled, showing a flash of white.

"Boy, that tooth is really showing up, isn't it?" Travis muttered, leaning closer.

"Plus two more coming in at the top. He's miserable. Can you blame him?"

Deke closed his eyes, wishing he could close his ears, as well. He didn't want to hear about babies and teething and pain. He didn't want any part of the whole scene.

"Are you okay?" Megan asked, her voice sounding concerned. Deke opened his eyes.

"Yeah. I'm wrestling with the granddaddy of all headaches at the moment, but I'll live through it."

Travis got up and walked over to the cabinet, found some pain medication and set it down in front of Deke along with a glass of water. "That should help."

He shook out a couple of tablets and swallowed them before murmuring his thanks.

"I'm a little concerned about this idea of Mollie's to help you out," Megan said, "but once you get to know Mollie, you'll discover that she has a mind of her own. She's quiet, but as stubborn as a mule."

"I don't really understand why she's offered to help me. Like you say, I don't know Mollie. Not really. I guess I know most of the kids in the county, either them or their folks, but I don't remember much about her."

Megan finished cleaning Danny's hands, hair, neck and face before she gave him a teething ring and returned her attention to Deke, saying, "Now that I've given her idea more thought, I realize that I shouldn't be surprised that she would offer to do something like this. Mollie is a natural-born homemaker. There's nothing she'd rather do than to putter around the kitchen trying new recipes, baking, sewing, that sort of thing... and she's been wonderful with Danny the little she's been home since he was born."

"But she's too young to be living there with me," Deke said pointedly. "It doesn't look right."

"I agree," Travis promptly added.

After another sip of coffee, Deke said, "The thing is, I've put myself into a bind of sorts. Having the neighbor ladies in and out of the house all the time was about driving me crazy. I finally exploded at 'em this morning, told 'em to get out, which of course they did. I'm really ashamed of myself, but you can't believe how peaceful and quiet it is around there now that they're gone. I'm just not used to all the ruckus. But I hadn't hired anybody to look after the baby. It was a dumb thing to do. I'm the first to admit it. That's when I remembered that Mollie came out a while back and offered to help me out. So I decided to take her up on her offer. The truth is, I don't know what I'm going to do without her."

"We could look after Jolene here, if you'd like," Megan said.

"No. Thank you, but she's my responsibility. I can't just farm her out like some unwanted puppy. Besides, you've got your hands full already." He looked over at Travis. "I want you to know that Mollie will be perfectly safe staying with me."

"If I didn't already know that, she wouldn't be over there right now," Megan said quietly. "This has nothing to do with you, personally, Deke, and you know it. But she does have her reputation to consider. She's really unaware of what talk can do, how much it can hurt."

Megan left the table and picked up the coffeepot, refilling their cups. "I'll go finish packing her things. It won't take much longer. That's another thing about Mollie. She's very organized and neat. You'll find it easy to get used to having her around."

Once she left the kitchen Deke muttered, "That's what's worrying me. She's a damn attractive woman. That's the last thing I need in my life at the moment."

"Thanks for being honest about it," Travis said with a half smile.

Deke got up abruptly and turned away. He walked over to the screen door and stared outside. "I've always lived by a strong code of honor, Travis, no matter what. Mollie will be as safe at my place as she's been here with you and Megan. I wish I could prevent any comments about the situation, but people being who and what they are, I know there's bound to be talk about us staying out at the ranch together. All I can say is, I'll do my best to find someone to come in and take over as soon as I can."

"If there's anything Megan or I can do for you, let me know," Travis said from behind him. "I'll go see if Megan's finished packing."

When Deke finally looked around, he was alone in the kitchen, except for the teething infant watching him steadily from across the room. His chest tightened. What was it about babies that got to a person so? Their wide-eyed gazes seemed to look straight through him, seeing the hollowness inside.

He didn't have anything to give. There was nothing left. And yet he was supposed to learn how to care for a child, how to nurture one. He shook his head. He was way over his head.

Patsy had been the one who'd suddenly decided that she wanted a child. Not him. Never him. He'd been adamant about starting a family. They'd talked about the idea of a family as soon as they'd discussed the possibility of marriage. He'd made his views quite clear. She'd agreed at the time, but later changed her mind without bothering to let him know. She'd been amused at his shock when she'd told him she was pregnant. As though she'd managed to pull off a wonderful practical joke. She'd ignored his anger and blithely made plans for the new arrival, laughing at him when he'd attempted to discuss how betrayed he felt about her decision to get pregnant without telling him of her intentions.

There were times when her laughter still rang in his ears, as though she were still amused at his predicament. He'd continued to drink to drown out the sounds, but nothing had worked.

Hiring Mollie was probably another mistake, but it certainly wouldn't be the first one he'd made. Marrying Patsy had been his biggest one. He'd paid for that one over and over.

From the looks of things, he'd be paying for the rest of his life.

Chapter Four

Mollie heard the truck coming up the lane and was waiting at the end of the walkway when Deke pulled in and parked. He wore mirrored aviator shades that concealed his gaze, but there was no ignoring the grim expression around his mouth and jaw.

Knowing her sister and brother-in-law, she had a hunch she knew why.

She watched him get out of the truck, then reach behind the seat and pull out the suitcase she used for college. Mollie drew in a deep breath and approached him. "Thank you for getting my things for me."

"You aren't going to be here long enough to use that much," he replied, stepping around her and continuing up the path.

"It's the only suitcase I have," she explained, following him into the house. "I doubt Megan packed for more than a few days."

He paused halfway down the hall and pushed open a door. The room was obviously a guest room that looked unused. He nodded toward another door. "The bathroom's through there. It opens into the other bedroom where the baby is. You'll be able to hear her from in here."

"Thank you."

He glanced around. "No need to thank me. I haven't done anything." He spun on his heel and disappeared from view but it didn't take long before she heard from him. "What the he—? What were you doing in here in my room?" he bellowed.

She followed the sound of his voice and found him standing in the middle of his now-clean bedroom. "Earning my living," she replied in a mild tone of voice.

She could see that he wanted to say more, much more, but was equally determined not to, for which she commended his restraint. She'd done nothing more than she'd said she would do.

"I have a roast in the oven. We'll be eating in another hour," she announced before turning away and leaving him standing there.

Deke knew he was in trouble and it didn't have anything to do with the fact that he now had a clean room, with fresh sheets on the bed and no doubt newly washed towels in his bathroom.

He wasn't ready to deal with all these changes. He couldn't handle it. Unfortunately he was being forced to.

He spun on his heel and strode down the hallway and out the door, ignoring the woman who now held his daughter in her arms. He had to get out of here.

He got back into his truck and took one of the ranch roads up into the hills where he could be guaranteed some solitude. He had to get away. He wasn't certain he could survive the next few weeks, much less the coming months and years.

Deke followed the road, which was little more than a rutted track up into the hills, following along a ledge that gave way to more hills dropping away in the distance.

At the top of one of the ridges he stopped and got out of the truck. He walked over to a large outcropping of stone and sat down. Now that he was here he wondered why he'd spent so much time hidden away in his room. This was where he belonged. Here was a place where he could breathe, where he could see for miles, where he could remember the past without being stifled by the pain.

His grandfather had worked for many long years to put this place together, taking any profits he made and investing in more land. His only son, Deke's father, had never shown an interest in the place. He'd gone into the service and never returned home.

Deke would never forget the first time he saw this land and the man who turned out to be his grandfather. He'd been little more than seven years old when his mother had taken him by bus from Greensboro, Mississippi, to Agua Verde, Texas. They had gotten off the bus in the small town and somehow she'd managed to find somebody to drive them out to the ranch.

The man he was today could better understand what had happened back then, but at the time the little boy had been confused and bewildered. All his mother had told him was that he was going to see his grandfather. Of course he'd been excited at first...eager, even, to meet a new relative. He'd never known his father. He'd only seen some blurry snapshots of him, taken before Deke was born.

He would never forget standing there in the driveway, holding his mother's hand, and watching the lean old man walk slowly toward them.

"Hello," his mother had said. "My name is Lena. You probably never heard of me but I've heard lots about you and this place." She looked around at the cluster of buildings surrounding the ranch yard. She tugged on Deke's hand, pulling him forward. "This is your grandson, Mr. Crandall. I named him Deke. Me and Roy got married just before he shipped out, even though he wasn't any too happy about it, but I wanted my baby to be legal and all and he is. I brought all the papers to show you. The military sent me an allotment for a while, then it stopped. I never heard from Roy again. Have you?"

His grandfather had looked at her for a long time without speaking, then he'd knelt in front of Deke so that they were eye level. He'd held out his hand to him, just as if he was another adult, and had said in a gruff voice, "I'm very pleased to meet you, son. You have no idea how glad. Nobody ever told me about you, I'm sorry to say."

He'd looked up at Deke's mother and said, "Young lady, you're welcome to stay here as long as you want, but if you ever decide to leave, just know that the boy stays here. This place is his heritage."

His mother had started crying then—big, heartbreaking sobs that had confused Deke even more. His grandfather had straightened and she had hugged him for the longest time, tears still pouring down her face.

"What's wrong, Mama? What did he say? Can't we stay, Mama?"

"Of course you can stay, son. Your mama's just tired, I expect. No doubt she's been struggling with a heavy load on her own for quite a spell." His grandfather had nodded toward the house. "Come on in and I'll show you where you'll be staying."

Deke had been preparing to go away to college before his grandfather ever explained to him the reasons behind what he'd witnessed that day. His mother had been told that she had inoperable cancer and she had done the only thing she knew to protect her little boy. Because of Roy's view of the place and his father, she hadn't been certain of her welcome, but she'd come anyway, determined to do whatever she could to provide for him.

All Deke had known growing up was that his mother had never seemed to have much energy and that as time went by she got thinner and thinner. His grandfather had taken her to several doctors but there hadn't been much of anything they could do for her. She'd managed to live until a few days past Deke's eleventh birthday.

He wouldn't have made it without his grandfather. Without his grandfather he wouldn't have this place, either. Deke had been in his senior year at Texas A & M when he got the call that his grandfather's heart had finally worn out. He'd gone to sleep one night and had never awakened.

Deke had graduated from college, getting the degree his grandfather had wanted for him, then he'd returned home to the ranch that was his legacy from the old man. He'd lived there alone in that old house for several years before he had met Patsy. She'd been everything he wasn't—warm and vivacious, filled with life and a love of excitement. Why hadn't it occurred to him at the time that the ranch offered very little in the way of excitement?

They'd been married almost a year before she told him the truth about her past, who she was, why she'd been willing to bury herself on a ranch. By then she'd given up pretending that he'd been anything more than a safe haven to run to. That's when he knew that there was something really wrong with him, something that people couldn't love. Of course his dad hadn't tried, and his mama had died. His granddad had done his best, but Deke knew, he just knew, that there must be something lacking in him that people sensed.

He'd left Patsy alone after that, pretty much. At least she'd finally decided not to lie to him anymore. She'd leave for a few months at a time, then return home, saying she missed him, saying she was ready to settle down for good. After a while she even insisted that she loved him. But he knew better by then.

After she told him she was pregnant, she kept saying that a baby was just what they needed to make their marriage work.

He knew better.

He didn't know anything about being a father. He'd never had one, even though his grandfather had meant everything in the world to him. In the most secret part of his heart, he'd lived with the fear that he was too much like his father. He couldn't handle the thought of bringing a child into the world, of being responsible for another person.

None of that mattered to Patsy, of course. The baby was already on the way.

She'd been so blasted determined to do things her way. As though having a child would make their relationship work better, would keep her from being so lonely away from the city lights and entertainment, would solve all their problems.

And now Patsy was gone. His grief had arisen out of guilt that he hadn't loved her enough, that he hadn't been capable of being the husband she wanted and needed. He'd let her down. He'd let himself down.

Now he was left with a baby girl to raise on his own. He'd never been so frightened in all his life.

Mollie O'Brien was right, though. He couldn't stay locked away in his room forever. He was too much of a coward to take his life and too afraid to live it. Living it meant making more mistakes, this time with an innocent child who would suffer from his poor judgment.

What was it they said about the sins of the fathers? Well, here was another generation of Crandalls, still suffering the sins of their fathers, and there wasn't a thing he could do about it.

The sun was setting by the time he turned his truck around and headed back to the ranch. Thank God he had a foreman who knew how to take care of the place. Otherwise he'd be in worse shape than he was. His grandfather had been an astute businessman and had made some wise investments over the years. Deke had never had to worry about the ranch paying for itself, even though it did.

Ranching would never make a person rich, but it was in his blood, just as it had been in his grandfather's. His grandfather had done everything he could for Deke. Somehow, Deke would have to do the same for his tiny daughter.

The problem was that at the moment he just didn't have any idea how.

Mollie was in the kitchen baking something when he stepped into the house. She glanced around and smiled at him. "You must be starved. Let me warm up your dinner" was all she said about the fact that he'd disappeared several hours before.

The funny thing was, he was hungry for the first time since he could remember. "I'll go get washed up" was all he replied before going through the doorway into the hall and on to his room.

The room still reflected its newly cleaned image. He had to admit to himself that he kind of liked it now that he was getting used to it. There was an unopened bottle of bourbon in his office. He might open it later to help him sleep, but in the meantime, he'd clean up a little and try some of Mollie's cooking. If it was as good as her coffee and biscuits, he'd really lucked out. She was going to make some lucky fellow a hell of a wife someday.

Deke couldn't sleep. He'd tossed and turned for hours, fighting the restless dreams that kept sweeping over him. After the last one he threw back the covers with a groan and sat up.

Times like this he wished he'd started smoking, but his grandfather had been so adamant about his not starting the habit that he'd never been tempted before now. He was fairly certain it was too late for him to find any real satisfaction from cigarettes.

Even though his mother's cancer had not been in her lungs, his grandfather had convinced him as a young boy that if cigarettes could cause that kind of suffering as well, he would leave them alone.

He'd started drinking after Patsy died, when he couldn't sleep, thinking it was better than taking prescription drugs, but now he wasn't so sure. He couldn't seem to sleep without it.

Without turning on a light he pulled on his jeans and stepped into the hallway to go to his office. He paused when he saw light coming from the baby's room. Taking a couple of silent steps, he stopped in front of the half-open door and peered inside.

Mollie was lifting the baby from her crib and giving her a bottle. He hadn't heard the baby. He was too far away with the door closed between them, but Mollie had obviously heard her stirring. He watched unseen as the woman he barely knew held his baby in her arms.

Only then did he realize that she wasn't wearing much of anything. She hadn't bothered to grab a robe. Instead she wore a sheer cotton nightshirt that stopped at midthigh in front and back, but came up higher on either side, barely covering her hips. It was sleeveless with a scooped neck. Her breasts were youthful—firm and full, their darker tips apparent through the thin material.

She sat down in the rocker, her movement calling his attention to her long, shapely legs. Only then did he realize that he was standing there like some sleazy voyeur ogling the woman he'd hired to take care of his infant daughter.

Taking care that she didn't see or hear him, he retreated to his room, thankful he was barefoot. Once closed, he leaned against the door. Damn. His heart was racing as though he'd been in a footrace, and he was more than a little aroused.

What in hell was he thinking of, standing there spying on her that way? Didn't he have an ounce of decency left in his body? Hadn't he just reassured her relatives that she was perfectly safe staying there with him?

Well, now he knew better. So he'd just have to do something about the situation immediately. Tomorrow he'd place an ad in all the newspapers within a hundred miles. He had to get permanent help as soon as possible.

Forgetting his original destination, Deke threw himself back on the bed and burrowed his head into the pillow. It was unfortunate that his dreams for the rest of the night gave him glimpses of long legs, full breasts and the shining sparks of red in a mass of tumbling dark hair.

Despite having to get up with the baby during the night, Mollie felt wonderfully rested when she awoke. Granted, it was the sounds of the baby that had pulled her out of a dreamless sleep, but she willingly went into the adjoining room and took care of her new charge.

Once again Jolene was wide-eyed and watching her every move.

"I'll never admit it to Megan, sugar," she said in a cooing voice, "but you are just about the prettiest baby I've ever seen, bar none. Of course, Danny doesn't need to be pretty 'cause he's a boy, but just to be on the safe side, let's keep my secret between the two of us, okay?''

Jolene waved one of her arms and gave an energetic double kick with her feet.

"Oh, aren't you smart! Just look at you go. I can't get over how alert you are and how wise you look, just like you're understanding every word I'm saying.''

Jolene made a little squeak and after much effort, a tiny coo.

"I was right. You're having a little trouble letting me know, but you understand everything, don't you?''

As soon as she fed the baby, Mollie took her into the kitchen and placed her in the bassinet out of the traffic area in the room. She put on coffee and began to make biscuits as well as fry up several strips of bacon. She would wait until Deke came into the kitchen before she prepared his eggs.

Mollie had no reason to suppose he'd come in, for that matter. Just because he'd stayed out of his room once he returned with her things the day before didn't mean that he didn't intend to continue to hibernate in there now that she was there to care for Jolene.

Everybody had their own way of dealing with pain. It didn't just go away because a person wished it to do so. She certainly wasn't going to judge the method he used, even though his bourbon consumption, if the empty bottles were any indication, concerned her. She'd heard about people trying to drown their sorrows but this was the first time she'd ever witnessed it.

Oh, well. That wasn't part of her concern. After dinner last night they had sat down and discussed her salary as well as her duties. Deke had been polite but distant.

Not that she blamed him. After all, he didn't know her. He'd probably be shocked if he ever learned that she used to have a tremendous crush on him. She'd be mortified if he or anyone else should ever find out, but there was little chance of that. She'd never shared that particular secret with anyone, not even her sisters.

Who would have believed back then that one day she would actually be living in the same house with him, taking care of his beautiful and bright daughter? It was strange the way things worked out sometimes.

She was taking the biscuits out of the oven when she heard a sound behind her. Since the baby was in the other direction, she knew it wasn't Jolene. Mollie straightened and looked around. Deke stood at the counter pouring himself some coffee.

He looked fresh from the shower, his hair still damp, newly shaved, wearing clean jeans, a chambray shirt and well-worn boots.

"Good morning," she said to his back. "You're about the quietest person I've ever been around. I never heard you come in." She removed the biscuits from the oven and placed them on top of the stove. "How would you like your eggs this morning?"

He gave her a brief glance then looked away. His gaze also avoided the area where Jolene lay sleeping. He sat down at the table and took a careful sip before replying, "Same as yesterday, I guess."

So he wasn't much of a morning person. Lots of people weren't. She felt blessed that she could hop out of bed and within minutes be wide-awake and ready to face her day. She remembered how Megan used to grumble at her cheerfulness. Oh, Megan was always up early, she had to be to take care of the chores, but she was a bear until she'd had at least two cups of coffee.

So Mollie, based on past experience, wisely chose not to make conversation with her new employer. Instead she carefully broke three eggs into the skillet and finished preparing his breakfast.

Once she'd set his plate in front of him, she made another one for herself. Then she sat down across from him and diligently ate, unobtrusively checking on the baby from time to time.

When he finished, Deke picked up his plate and took it to the sink where he rinsed it and placed it in the dishwasher. He refilled his cup and sat down again before he spoke.

"Mollie?"

She'd gotten so used to the silence that her heart leaped in surprise. "Yes?" she asked, taking a quick sip of coffee to wash down the bite of toast she'd almost swallowed wrong.

"I want you to know that I appreciate your immediate response to my call yesterday," he began in his soft-spoken drawl. "The thing is, I've had some time to think about it. I guess I really blew it yesterday with those ladies and I want you to know that I'm grateful that you came to my rescue." He paused and sipped his coffee while she warily watched him. "But after sleeping on it, I realize that Megan and Travis are right. This isn't going to work, you being here with me like this."

She waited and when he didn't say anything more, she said, "I don't understand. I thought we discussed this last night and you were agreeable to my staying until you could find somebody permanent. What did I do? If I've offended you in some way, just tell me. I can follow any routine you prefer. I can stay out of your way, I can—"

"No, it's not any of that." Mollie wasn't sure that she wasn't imagining it, but she could almost believe that Deke was blushing. She stayed silent and he began to haltingly say, "You and I know that you're much too young for me, but the fact remains that you're a very attractive woman and I— Well, I just can't—" He shook his head. This time there was no doubt that his cheeks were ruddier and that he was very uncomfortable.

What was he saying here? That he found her attractive? Mollie fought not to give away her reaction to his words.

"Anyway," he went on after clearing his throat, "I realized last night that I've put us both in a rather uncomfortable situation. I'm really sorry about that." Once again he cleared his throat. "Until I can find someone to stay permanently, I'm going to be spending my nights out in the cabin with the single men." She could see that it was an effort for him to meet her gaze. "I'm really sorry for getting you involved in all this."

Her gaze remained steady. "I'm not. I'm happy that I can help. I'm just sorry you're uncomfortable about my being here."

"It's nothing you've done, Mollie, believe me."

"It's okay. I understand." She got up from the table and began to gather the dishes. "I hope you find somebody that will be good to Jolene."

He nodded abruptly. "So do I." He pushed away from the table, grabbed his hat and headed toward the door. "Thanks for understanding," he said before almost racing to his truck.

Molly watched him, shaking her head. Men were really funny creatures. Yesterday he was begging her to come help. Today he could hardly wait to get rid of her.

Guess she'd never understand them.

Chapter Five

A week before Christmas vacation was due to begin, Mollie pushed open the door to her dorm room and dispiritedly crossed to her desk, tossing her books on the paper-covered surface. With a sigh she slumped down onto the side of the bed and stared at the papers scattered across the desk's surface.

"I hate this," she muttered to herself. "I really hate it."

Her fall class schedule included several business classes—statistics, finance, economics—all of which she was failing or near failing. Why? Because she had little or no interest in business.

So why was she taking the courses?

That was the question of the century. Why had she allowed Megan to talk her into majoring in a subject for which she had no aptitude nor interest?

Partly it was because Megan had always taken the lead in their relationship. The six-year edge made an enormous difference while they were growing up, not to the mention the fact that it had been Megan's strong determination to fight for the family unit that had kept them together.

So she had felt that she owed Megan something... that she owed it to Megan to go on to college, since Megan hadn't gone. Now that Megan and Travis could afford to pay for college, neither one of them had asked Mollie if she wanted to go, or what subjects she might want to take. Instead it was a foregone conclusion that Mollie and Maribeth would have the opportunity that Megan never had.

So here she was, Mollie thought with disgust, in her third year of school, hating every minute of it. The next biggest question was, what did she intend to do about it? There were options, of course. She could change her major, or she could drop out of school entirely. Since Megan wouldn't be any too happy with that particular choice, Mollie knew she would have to come up with something else she could do with herself, instead.

An image immediately formed in her head of those few short weeks last summer when she'd taken care of Jolene and attempted to provide Deke a place where he could begin the healing process.

She leaned back on her pillow, remembering those days with a smile. Despite all his intentions, Deke had discovered that it wasn't all that easy to find a permanent replacement for Mollie, which gave her the opportunity to truly fall in love with Jolene as well as her daddy.

Jolene was so easy to love. Her father much less so. Jolene was a happy baby most of the time. She just wanted her needs met immediately, that was all. In exchange, Jolene did whatever she could to entertain Mollie—cooing, grabbing on to her hair or nose, chuckling every time Mollie tickled her tummy.

Jolene would be so different now—almost nine months old. Danny had been walking by that age. She wondered if Jolene had decided to explore her world so quickly?

Mollie also wondered about Deke. Had he changed his attitude toward Jolene, shown any more interest in her? She hoped so. While Mollie had been there on the ranch, Deke had ignored them both. Once he'd left the sanctuary of his room, he'd spent all of his waking hours working with his men on the ranch or buried behind his accounts in his office.

His nights were always spent across the ranch yard in the bunkhouse.

He did little more than nod at Mollie whenever he was brought face-to-face with her, and it was obvious that he would have avoided those encounters if possible.

Whenever she tried to talk to him about Jolene he would leave the room. He never looked at his daughter or asked about her.

So how could she possibly love a man like that? she wondered. But she knew. Oh, yes, she understood why... because she saw his pain, no matter how much he tried to hide it. She saw the agony that he was going through every time Jolene wailed, or squealed, or blew bubbles. Jolene represented a loss he couldn't come to terms with, and he couldn't bear to be reminded.

Eventually he'd found a woman from Austin who agreed to move to Agua Verde—a Mrs. Franzke. She was a very pleasant woman and Mollie knew that Jolene no doubt had adapted quickly to yet another face in her life, but it had taken Mollie most of the summer to adjust to not seeing Deke and Jolene on a daily basis. Thank God Danny had been there for her. She'd spent the remainder of the summer helping Megan with Danny in an attempt to get on with her life.

She envied Megan, having a husband and son, being where she wanted to be, doing what she wanted to do. If Mollie had her choice... but exactly what would she choose? At the moment all she could do was to study harder in order not to flunk out of school. Perhaps after the Christmas break she would look into switching majors.

Instead of doing the assignments she'd been given earlier, she curled into her pillow and dozed off, awakening only when someone tapped on her door.

"Mollie?" It was Sharon from across the hall. "You in there?"

Mollie sat up. "Come on in, Sharon. I must have fallen asleep."

Sharon peeked around the door, grinning. "You've got a caller downstairs."

Mollie was puzzled by Sharon's tone of voice and her expression. "Who?"

"I didn't ask. But whoever he is, I've gotta tell you, he's got every gal in the place finding some reason to wander through the reception area. Talk about a hunk."

Mollie grabbed her hairbrush. "Does he have a woman with him? Maybe it's Megan and Travis."

"Uh-uh. All alone, looking a little harried with all the attention he's getting. He's rolled and unrolled the brim on his Stetson so many times, it'll never be the same."

Mollie froze, her eyes widening. "Deke? Could it possibly be—?"

"Only one way to find out, gal. Go check him out."

It couldn't be Deke. Why would he be here? She hadn't heard anything from him since she'd left the ranch at the end of June. But who else could it be? She wasn't dating anyone these days.

When she walked into the reception area she saw him with his back to the room, staring out the window. There was no mistaking those broad shoulders or the lean, muscled back and buttocks. Her heart was working overtime in an effort to get blood to her head. Even so, she felt light-headed at the sight of him.

"Deke?"

He spun around at the sound of her voice. He hadn't removed his sheepskin-lined denim jacket, although it hung open, revealing the plaid flannel shirt beneath. He clutched his hat in one hand while his other hand was fisted. He jammed it into his coat pocket as he strode toward her.

"Is there somewhere private where we could talk?" he asked, without bothering with a polite greeting. Yep, it was Deke, all right. He looked around the busy area with an expression bordering on desperation, reminding Mollie of his behavior last summer around the group of women who had taken care of Jolene. "If you have time," he added as an obvious afterthought to the social niceties of polite behavior.

Mollie carefully hid the smile that was hovering around her mouth. "I've got time," she replied, astounded at how thrilled she was to see him again. Here she had thought she'd managed to get over her feelings for the man, darn it. Now all she could do was try not to embarrass herself with her eagerness. "Why don't we go for coffee? There's a place not too far from here where we won't be disturbed."

"You'll need your coat" was all he said. Definitely a man of few words, but she managed to detect a slight relaxation in the taut lines around his mouth.

She nodded. "I'll be right back." She waited until she was out of his line of sight before racing to the stairs, taking them two at a time, and running down the hallway to her room. She wasn't in the least surprised to see Sharon stick her head out of her room.

"Well?"

"He's a friend from home." She tossed out the answer as she grabbed her jacket.

"Yummy. Wish I had friends like that. Are you going to introduce him around?"

"He's shy."

Sharon laughed knowingly. "Oh, I'll just bet he is!" Her last words followed Mollie as she dashed back to the stairs.

Mollie had given the first excuse she could think of, but as she returned to Deke she realized that it was the truth, at least where women were concerned. Why else would he have felt so ill at ease with the women who'd come to tend to Jolene? If she hadn't been so persistent the day she'd gone out to see him, he would have avoided her, as well. In the end, she had been the means to save him from the other women.

As she approached him for the second time today, she realized that once again her presence would rescue him from another gathering of interested females, several of whom were attempting to draw him out in conversation. They were having little success, however, and Mollie knew it was time for her to get him out of there.

She moved to his side and looped her arm through his. "Ready?" she asked brightly, just as though she was used to taking such liberties with him, when the truth was she had never been this close to him before.

He glanced down at her, his expression a mixture of relief and surprise, no doubt startled by her unaccustomed familiarity with him. With a curt nod, he jammed his poor hat back on his head and headed toward the door in his long-legged stride. Once there, he shoved the door open and waited for her to walk through. Mollie slipped her hands into the pockets of her coat before she was tempted to touch him again.

He looked so good to her after all this time. He had regained some of his weight, so that he didn't look quite so gaunt, although there were new lines on his face. His hair was still overlong, as though he couldn't be bothered to have it trimmed.

Mollie led the way to the student hangout off campus waiting for him to speak. After a prolonged silence she mentally shrugged and asked, "How's Jolene?"

"She's okay," he replied gruffly. "Not sick or anything."

"I bet she's really grown. I've thought about her over the months, wondering what she looks like now."

Once again she waited, but he showed no signs of grabbing his wallet and revealing an abundance of baby pictures for her to admire.

She gave a tiny shrug of acceptance, then asked, "And Mrs. Franzke?"

He let out a deep sigh of frustration. "Oh, *she's* all right. It's just..." He seemed to run out of words and breath at the same time. He adjusted his hat, pulling the brim down even lower over his eyes. Uh, oh. Something was definitely wrong, but then she'd known that. Why else would he have turned up here on the UT campus looking for her?

"What is it, Deke? Why are you here? What's wrong?"

He just shook his head, more in weariness than in denial and said nothing more until they reached the café. The place was cavernous, but there weren't many people inside at the moment. After all, it was Friday afternoon, with only a few days before the Christmas holidays and most people were either studying, shopping, or getting ready for a date. Since Molly had already made all her gifts and had only one more test before school was out, she had not lied when she told Deke she had time for him.

They found a booth in the back and waited for their coffee to be delivered without speaking. Mollie knew that Deke would answer her questions, but in his own time. There was no pushing the man, that much she'd learned.

So she waited.

"Mrs. Franzke's sister had a stroke a few days ago," he finally said, not looking at her. "She's doing better, but once she's released from the hospital she's not going to be able to look after herself any longer. Mrs. Franzke feels that she has no choice but to move in and help."

"Ah," Mollie said, immediately understanding why Deke had shown up on her doorstep. At the least the guy was predictable! "So you need me to take care of Jolene until you can find someone else," she concluded for him. "Well, that shouldn't be a problem. I'll be coming home next Wednesday for a couple of weeks, which should give you time to—"

"Mollie, I need your help." His voice sounded desperate and strangled, as though he was trying to remember lines he'd been rehearsing but hated having to give.

Hadn't he just heard what she'd said? Without conscious thought, she reached across the scarred table and touched the back of his hand with her fingertips. "It's okay, Deke," she said in a soothing voice. "I can help you out. It won't be a problem for me."

He studied her hand as though he'd never seen one before and she glanced down, seeing how her neatly shaped nails and pale skin contrasted with his scarred knuckles and callused fingers. He slipped his hand from beneath hers as though he'd been made uncomfortable by her touch.

After gripping his hands in a tight clasp in front of him, Deke shifted on the bench seat of the booth and met her inquiring gaze with narrowed eyes. "Before you so freely volunteer, maybe you should hear what I'm going to ask of you."

Mollie folded her hands in her lap. She'd been trying to ease his tension, but it hadn't worked. So she smiled at him when she would have preferred to kick him in the shins. Why did he have to make the most simple conversation such a strain?

He looked away from her, then reached for his coffee. After taking a gulp of the hot liquid he said, "Ever since we got the call about Mrs. Franzke's sister, I've

known that I was going to have to do something about
my situation. I was damn lucky to be able to find
someone like Mrs. Franzke and I know it. Nobody's
interested in living out so far in the boonies these days.
Not people qualified to care for children, anyway. There
are too many jobs in cities where they can enjoy their
time off doing stuff besides staring out at the rolling
hills and listening to the howls of coyotes."

Mollie grinned. She couldn't help it. He sounded so
disgusted. "I never minded," she stated softly.

His gaze met hers for a moment, then danced away.
"Yeah, I know. I guess that's because you were raised
on a ranch, grew up in that kind of place, know what to
expect."

"There's another reason, Deke, besides my background. I happen to love your little daughter. She's easy
to love, you know."

A muscle flexed in his jaw but he didn't say anything. Instead he straightened in the booth, pressing his
shoulders against the back. After a weighty silence,
Deke rubbed his forehead as though he might be dealing with a headache. She could tell this interview, if she
could call it that, was tough for him, but she didn't
know what she could say or do to make it any easier.

His voice was gruff when he spoke again. "I can't
have a young woman like you working for me. We've
already covered that territory last summer."

Now she really was confused. If he wasn't here to offer her a job, even on a temporary basis, then what did

he want? Mollie felt unnerved without understanding why. What could Deke want from her?

"I want to make you an offer, Mollie," he said through his clenched jaw. "I've been thinking about this for a while. You'll probably think I'm crazy, and maybe I am. I don't know much about anything anymore. Nothing in my life has gone as I thought it would, so now I'm grasping at straws. Don't think I don't know that."

She was even more unnerved by his grim expression. "All right," she managed to say.

"I'm asking you to marry me, Mollie," he began and continued to speak in that deep voice of his, but Mollie heard no more after those first few words.

Deke was asking her to marry him? Deke? Asking her? For a moment she was convinced the room had started to sway before she realized that his words had put her into shock. She stared at him, only then realizing that he was still talking and she hadn't heard another thing he'd said.

"I'm sorry," she managed to blurt out. "I'm sorry, but I wasn't keeping up with what you were saying. Did I hear you correctly? Did you just ask me to marry you?"

Now it was Deke's turn to look taken aback. He frowned, as though his carefully rehearsed words had suddenly deserted him.

"Yeah," he drawled, grabbing his cup and draining it before adding, "that's what I'm trying to say here."

"I don't understand," she finally mumbled. "I mean, we really don't know each other very well. You've never given me any reason to think that you—" She swallowed, unable to find the words to describe the usual sentiments that went along with a marriage proposal.

"I know I'm doing this all wrong, but I've never proposed to anybody before, besides the fact that this isn't really a—"

"What do you mean, you've never proposed before? You were married to—"

"Yeah, I know. But I wasn't the one who suggested getting married. She did. She convinced me that nothing would make her happier, so I kinda went along with it."

He was definitely blushing, which eased her discomfort a little.

"Is this your way of protecting my reputation so I can take care of Jolene?"

"So what if it is? People get married for all kinds of reasons, not just because they think they're in love with each other." He shoved his hand through his hair. "You don't need to tell me how unfair I'm being to you. You're too young for me. I know that. You've got your whole life ahead of you. You're a beautiful woman, intelligent— It was a stupid idea, I see that now." He looked around as though wanting to leave. "Why don't we just forget all about it, forget I said anything. Put it down to not enough sleep and working too hard." He looked back at her. "You ready to go? I need to head back to the ranch. There's no reason for me to—"

"Deke?"

He eyed her warily. "Yeah?"

"Can we talk about this offer of yours for a minute or two before you withdraw it, please?"

"What do you mean, withdraw it?"

"Well, you haven't given me a chance to even think about it before you've decided it's a bad idea."

"I shouldn't have said anything."

"I'm glad you did, Deke," she said, deliberately reaching out and taking his hand, clasping it firmly in hers. "I'm glad you trust me enough, have faith in my abilities enough to want me to be a full-time mother to Jolene."

She could feel the tension in his hand but refused to let go. She needed to touch him. Needed to feel his warmth, to know that whether or not he loved her, or wanted her in the way a man wants a woman, that Deke Crandall needed her in his life.

"It wouldn't be like a real marriage or anything," he blurted out, his eyes looking everywhere but at her. He cleared his throat. "What I mean is, if you're seriously considering my offer I want you to know that I don't expect you to pretend to love me or anything like that."

"I see," she said, watching him closely.

"You'd still have your own room, if you wanted it. I...uh...know that sounds like a strange way to go into a marriage, but sometimes maybe it's better to be straight with each other up-front...and not pretend feelings we don't have.''

''A marriage of honesty, is that it?''

''Well, yeah, at least we don't have to pretend with each other.'' He studied her for several moments in silence before adding, ''I'm way too old for you, honey, don't think I don't know that. And what I'm suggesting is almost criminal, because I'm stealing your youth.''

She smiled. ''That's a little dramatic, don't you think? You aren't stealing anything. Whatever I decide, it will be my choice.'' She released his hand and leaned back in her seat. ''I want to be as honest as I can with you, Deke. I can't imagine anything I would rather do than to live at your ranch with you and care for Jolene.'' She gave a little chuckle. ''I'm really not into all this higher learning, I don't mind admitting to you. It's just that I never thought you'd insist that we be married in order for me to live there.''

The waitress came by and refilled their cups. Deke cupped his hands around the hot mug and studied the steaming liquid, allowing the silence to draw out between them once more.

When he looked up at her, his eyes seemed to shoot off sparks of green fire. ''I'm not going to lie to you and tell you that I'm making this offer just because of Jolene, because I'm not. But she is a large part of why I decided to marry again. I'd also planned to wait a while, at least until next summer, before mentioning it to you.

This thing with Mrs. Franzke has thrown everything into turmoil.''

Mollie couldn't believe what she was hearing.

"Then why did you decide on me?''

He rubbed his nose, then scratched his jaw. "I—uh—can't seem to get you out of my mind. I'm not going to pretend that I'm not attracted to you...because I am. For the past six months I've been telling myself that it was just what I was going through last spring that made you seem to be the only bright spot in my life. But it's more than that, Mollie. Even though you were only at the ranch for a few weeks, you left your touch there. Everywhere I look around the place, I see something that reminds me of you, and the time you were living there.''

Mollie couldn't believe her ears. Was it possible that Deke was as attracted to her as she was to him?

When she didn't comment, he went on in a low voice. "I've been trying to convince myself all this time that you're what Jolene needs." He cleared his throat. "But being around you reminds me of some of my needs, as well.'' In a rush of words, he explained, "That was the trouble I was having last summer. I didn't want to take advantage of the situation, or make you feel that I'd gotten you out there under false pretenses, but I discovered quick enough that you have a very strong effect on me." His gaze flickered back to meet hers. "I want you to know that I would never force myself on you or anything like that." The tips of his ears glowed red. "It would be your choice if, at a later date, you maybe wanted to have a real marriage with me. I promise you right now that I would never mistreat you in any way. I would always show you respect as my wife and the mother of my child regardless of what happens or doesn't happen between us.''

A lump formed in her throat, she was so touched by his words. Here was this man, so big and tough, trying to reassure her. She had known that there were depths to the man not easily seen. Otherwise, he would not have been in so much pain.

She didn't want to make too much over the fact that he had decided to ask her of all the women he knew to marry him. From his point of view, it was a sensible choice, since he'd already seen her in his home and caring for his child.

What gave her hope was his telling her that he was attracted to her, despite himself. Hearing him speak of his needs made her tingle. He was determined to be honest about his feelings. She wondered how he would feel if he knew that she was already halfway in love with him? If he knew that, would he be so eager to have her as his wife?

What he was suggesting was more than she ever expected him to offer, but was less than what she wanted from him. Could she make do with what he proposed?

She gazed across the table at him and smiled. Deke Crandall had talked more to her today than during all the time they'd spent together last summer. Now he sat there watching her in silence, as though he had run out of words.

"Deke," she began, feeling her way. "This is much too important a decision for me to make without giving it some thought."

"I know. Talking about it makes it seem really farfetched."

"No," she replied firmly. "It sounds very sensible and practical. I understand your reasons and I appreciate your being candid with me." She folded her arms and leaned on the table. "I know you said that you needed to get back, but I was wondering if you'd let me sleep on your suggestion overnight? If you would stay in town tonight, maybe we could meet for breakfast in the morning."

"You mean you're seriously considering my offer?"

His obvious surprise made her grin. All right, so it wasn't the most romantic proposal she'd ever heard about, but she was far from saying no to the possibility.

Mollie wasn't going to pretend that she wasn't intrigued by his offer. All right. More than intrigued. Nothing like this had ever happened to her before. It was as if someone had listened to her childhood prayers and dreams and was now offering them back to her.

The problem was, she was no longer a child. Any decision she made would have a profound effect on each of them as well as on Jolene. She had to think all of this through very carefully...unemotionally...rationally, and not be influenced by the look in his eyes or her regrettably strong reaction to him.

"I'm not sure I'll have an answer by tomorrow, but I promise to give the idea considerable thought." She glanced around. "In the meantime, are you interested in ordering something to eat? They make the best hamburgers and fries here you've ever eaten... just dripping with all kinds of fat and cholesterol."

He lifted one of his eyebrows. "Is that supposed to be a recommendation?"

She grinned. "They're the most delicious thing you've ever tasted, I'll guarantee you that much."

He looked around and saw that while they'd been talking the room had gradually filled up. "Now that I think about it, I haven't had anything since breakfast. Sure. Let's go ahead and order."

Mollie hoped that she had convinced him that an unexpected marriage proposal was a common day occurrence to her, one that she could blithely file away to consider at a later date.

At least he was considerably more relaxed now than when she'd first seen him. Why, he'd almost smiled at her enthusiasm for her menu choice. *That's it,* she reminded herself. *Keep it light. At the very least, he's offering you the possibility of a friendship with him. He admires you. He's also attracted to you. There were worse things than that on which to base marriage.*

Don't think about it now. You've bought yourself some time. She forced herself to smile at him while he gave their order to the admiring waitress. If Deke intended to marry in order to provide Jolene with a stable home life, and if she decided not to marry him,

Mollie had a hunch there would be plenty of women who would jump at the chance.

Would she—at some later date—be able to live with the knowledge of all she'd given up when it was too late to change her mind?

Did she have the courage to accept what he offered in the hope that someday it would grow into something more?

Chapter Six

Mollie opened her sleep-starved eyes and foggily focused on the digital clock beside her bed. It was just past three o'clock in the morning.

She groaned.

This had to be the longest night she'd ever spent. She kept dozing off and waking up, tossing and turning in an effort to get comfortable. It was useless for her to try to rest. Every time she fell asleep she dreamed the craziest dreams. She wasn't certain if she even wanted to go back to sleep.

By the time she'd left Deke at the front door to her dorm, she'd known how foolish it would be for her to enter into a loveless marriage, regardless of the mitigating circumstances. She wanted a marriage like Megan's. Travis obviously worshiped his wife. Mollie had hoped to be able to have the same kind of marriage someday.

However, Deke was offering her something considerably less.

Would being married to her childhood romantic ideal be enough for her? What if she discovered too late that it wasn't?

After weighing all the reasons, pro and con, her logical, orderly mind told her to forget about his proposal. It would never work and she could quite possibly end up being very unhappy.

So. There it was. She'd made her decision.

Hadn't she?

If so, then why didn't she feel better?

Because every time she closed her eyes she could see Deke's seductive eyes staring at her with reproach... or she would hear a baby crying on and on...and no one was responding.

She punched her pillow. It wasn't her problem. Just because she'd had a crush on the guy most of her life didn't have anything to do with reality. The reality was that he could very easily break her heart if she attempted to get closer to him than the boundaries he'd set between them.

So...now that she'd wisely dealt with the issue, she could go back to sleep.

Sure. Just like that, she could forget that Deke Crandall needed her, that he was giving her a chance to live with him, to get to know him better, to help him learn

how to live again, how to love again...if she had the
courage to try.

She pulled the pillow over her head and held it against
her ears. What a ridiculous idea. How could she teach
him anything? What did she know?

She knew how to love. She'd been given years of in-
struction by example...from her parents and from her
sisters. Maybe Deke hadn't had the benefit of similar
teachings. What, after all, did she really know about
him?

Besides, he'd obviously been deeply in love with his
wife, hadn't he? That had to count for something.

Slowly she withdrew her head and sat up on the side
of the bed. This was getting her nowhere. Why was she
having such an argument with herself? What was this all
about? Why couldn't she make up her mind?

It was then she understood what was happening. Her
head was arguing with her heart and neither one was
willing to back down. She could list all the logical, rational reasons against accepting Deke's offer...or she
could admit, at least to herself, that there was nothing
in the whole wide world she wanted more than to marry
Deke, to be his wife in every way, and to be a part of
Jolene's life.

As long as she was being so blasted honest with herself, she also wanted to give him more children. She
shivered, thinking about the possibility of sharing his
bed, of making love to him.

Once again Mollie stretched out on her bed, pulling
the covers up to her chin, and stared at the ceiling. She'd

never thought of herself as anything but practical, down-to-earth and rational. This time, none of that was enough. This time, she had to believe in something that wasn't tangible, but was real, nevertheless.

Despite all the evidence pointing to the contrary, Mollie knew that she would never know any peace unless she found the courage to go with her heart.

Mollie was watching for Deke the next morning from the reception area window. She stepped outside just as he approached the door.

A blustery norther had blown in earlier that morning. She pulled up the hood of her jacket and noted that he'd turned his collar up and his hat brim down.

He looked surprised to see her waiting. "Were you watching for me?" he asked warily. "Or hoping to sneak away before I showed up?" She could see a glint of amusement in his eyes.

"I thought I would save you the trial of being the object of everyone's interest inside." She stuck her hands into her coat jacket.

He slipped his arm through hers. "I didn't know I was that easy to read."

She grinned. "I remembered how you reacted to the women at your house last summer."

He rolled his eyes. "Please don't remind me. I'm only now getting some of them to speak to me again. I was way out of line and had to do some mighty tough apologizing."

"Good for you. A little humility is good for the soul. Builds character."

He nodded toward his truck. "I thought we might take the truck, if that's okay with you."

"Anything to get out of this wind." She walked arm and arm with him to where he'd left the truck and got inside. It was still toasty warm, and as soon as he started the engine, the heater kicked out a gust of hot air across her feet and ankles.

"We may get some snow before the day's out," he said, backing out of the parking space.

"I guess you're eager to get home, aren't you?"

"Yeah. I never like being away for long. Guess I'm a homebody."

"That's something we have in common," she stated quietly. "It was very tough for me to adjust to being here at school."

He was quiet for several blocks before he said, "How much longer do you have to go before you graduate?"

"If I pass all my subjects this semester, another year and a half."

"It makes sense you'd want to see it through," he offered. She could only nod.

Neither one said anything else until after they reached the famous A-shaped building that was known for serving breakfasts around the clock. They gave their orders to the waitress and Mollie immediately sipped her coffee without looking at Deke again. She didn't have to, since her first glance at him this morning seemed to have noted the changes in him from the evening before.

He looked more rested, as though the hardest part for him had been finding a way to put his offer into words. The lines around his mouth weren't as severe, and he'd mentioned that he was hungry.

"You look a little tired this morning," he finally said. "Were you studying late last night?"

She made a face. A gentleman wouldn't have been so quick to point out her pale face and the circles beneath her eyes. Ah well, so much for looking for a gentleman.

"I've got one more final before the holidays," she replied truthfully enough, even though it had nothing to do with her looking as though she'd stayed awake all night.

"Mmm" was all he said before finishing his first cup of coffee and pouring another one from the carafe left by the waitress. He'd practically inhaled the first cup.

Deke leaned back in his chair and studied her, as though he were meeting her for the first time. Self-conscious, she pushed a lock of hair behind her ear. When she forced herself to meet his gaze, he gave her a lopsided smile.

"You don't have to say anything, you know," he said softly. "I never should have made such a crazy suggestion yesterday. Put it down to worry, overwork, not enough sleep and skipping too many meals."

What relief, was Mollie's first thought. *I don't have to say anything. He understands. Thank God. I don't have to explain or—* "So you're withdrawing your offer," she blurted out, sounding irritated. What in the world was the matter with her?

It didn't help that his smile moved into a slow, definitely sexy, grin. "If I didn't know better, I'd swear you were disappointed," he teased.

"Of course not! It's just that—" She glanced at him, then away. "I just worry about Jolene, that's all."

His smile disappeared. "So do I."

"So you're going to probably look around until you find a woman you really want to marry, right? Not somebody like me who you still see as some kind of schoolgirl who doesn't know her own mind or—"

"Whoa! Whoa! Wait a minute. What's going on here? I was just trying to help us over an awkward moment or two, that's all."

"Oh." She studied her hands, realigned her coffee mug on its paper doily before casually saying, "But you don't really want a wife. You're wanting to provide a stable home for Jolene."

"True enough. It does seem odd, now that we're talking about it, that I'd even consider getting married again. You'd think I would learn, huh? One disaster was enough."

"Disaster?"

He sighed and shook his head. "Patsy never thought I was much of a husband. I guess she was right. I didn't know the first thing about making a woman happy. Still don't. All I know is ranching. Arranging a marriage between us was strictly for your protection. Very selfishly, I wanted you to be willing to stay with Jolene, that's all." He looked away, no longer meeting her gaze. "I apologize for coming up with such a harebrained idea."

"What if I agreed to it?" she asked slowly. "What then?"

He had his coffee cup halfway to his mouth when she spoke and he froze, looking as though he'd been caught in suspended animation. Slowly he moved his gaze from his cup until he was staring at her for a long, silent moment.

Deke very carefully set the cup back on the table. "Are you kidding me?" His voice sounded gruff and strained.

"I'm willing to marry you, Deke, for however long you want it to last, for whatever reason you want to put on it...to look after Jolene...to protect my reputation...whatever."

There was no sign of the relaxed and smiling man now. "But why, Mollie? I should have been taken out and shot for coming up with the idea in the first place."

Mollie got a reprieve from having to come up with an immediate answer by the arrival of their breakfasts. She'd already forgotten what she'd ordered and stared at her plate as though she recognized nothing there.

She ignored his question while she carefully cut up her ham, seasoned her eggs and sipped her orange juice. When she glanced over at him he was already eating, so obviously this conversation hadn't disturbed his appetite any.

In fact, Deke waited until the waitress cleared their plates before he refilled their cups and faced her once again.

"Why would you be willing to leave school now and marry me?"

She lifted her chin slightly. "Maybe I've always wanted to get married and yours was the first offer."

He chuckled and shook his head. "Somehow I doubt that."

"Or maybe I've just been waiting all these years for you to notice that I've grown up," she said more slowly.

He raised an eyebrow at that one. "What do you mean? I didn't even know you before last summer, and you looked grown up enough to me then."

"Not really. You thought I was a high school student." When he didn't comment, she said, "Actually, we met many years ago when I was just a kid. You were breaking a horse one day when my dad and I came out to your ranch. It was when your grandfather was still alive."

His brows drew together slightly, as though he was searching his memory. Finally he shook his head. "I'm sorry. I don't remember."

"No reason for you to. But I feel like I've known you all my life."

"That isn't a very good reason to decide to marry me."

"Like you said," she stated in a casual tone, "it isn't like it's a real marriage offer, with love on either side. I'd be there to look after Jolene."

He stared at her quizzically. "Surely you want more than that out of a relationship."

She folded her hands and forced herself to meet his intent gaze. "Well, if it would make you feel any better, we could always have an understanding that when I meet someone I would like to have a real marriage with, I could tell you. Would that work?" She fought to keep her face composed as she waited for his reaction.

She was pleased by his frown. He didn't like that idea very much, which she considered to be a good sign.

"I guess that would work," he said after a long silence.

"So when do you want to do this?"

His brows went up. "You sound like you're in a hurry."

"Not me. You're the one who has to replace Mrs. Franzke. I don't see any reason to come back to school after the holidays, so I think we should plan a small wedding between Christmas and New Year's."

"Well, uh, I'd been thinking that— Well, if we did actually decide to get married...that we could do what Patsy and I did and just go to the courthouse to get married."

She was already shaking her head. "No. I want my family to be there. And I want to wear the gown that Megan was married in. It's a family tradition for us girls."

"What do you think your family's going to say about us suddenly deciding to get married? They're pretty protective of you."

"They just want me to be happy."

Silence stretched between them. "So do I, Mollie. I don't want to take advantage of you in any way."

She smiled. "Don't worry about it. I won't let you."

"Mary Katherine O'Brien! Have you completely lost your cotton-pickin' mind? Where is your head these days? I thought you'd gone bonkers last summer and that was for a summer baby-sitting job. But this! What could you be thinking of!"

Mollie, Megan and Maribeth were wrapping Christmas packages in the living room while Danny played in his toy-filled playpen. He threw one of his stuffed animals down and pulled himself up, peering over the side to see what had his mama so riled.

"I don't remember your asking me or Maribeth whether or not you should marry Travis, and you managed to pull that one off in a hurry."

"Not in less than two weeks! And besides, Travis and I— Well, we—"

"You always professed to hate Travis with a great deal of vehemence Megan, me-girl."

"Exactly! And I clearly recall how upset you were when you found out I'd agreed to marry him!"

"I see. So this is payback time, is it?"

"Of course not!"

"Then why are you so upset?"

"Because you don't know Deke Crandall, that's why! At least I grew up with Travis. Except for those few weeks you spent caring for Jolene last summer, you've never been around him."

"True."

"Well, then," she said in her most reasonable tone of voice. "Don't you want to get to know him better?"

Mollie gave her sister a very wicked grin. "Don't worry. I fully intend to... after we're married."

"You know perfectly well that's not what I'm talking about!" She glanced at Maribeth who was grinning. "And you could be helping me out here, you know."

Maribeth shrugged. "It's none of my business."

Mollie leaned over and hugged her younger sister. "Thank you, thank you, thank you. Now all we have to do is convince big sister that she doesn't have to concern herself, as well."

Megan wadded up a piece of wrapping paper and threw it at her. "All right. So I'm a busybody. So sue me."

"I just want you to quit worrying about me, okay? Please? If I'm making a mistake, it will be my mistake and I'll live with it."

"But he's too old for you!"

"Who says? I think he's the perfect age for me...and the perfect height for me...and the perfect—"

"Ah, love," Maribeth sighed theatrically, clutching her chest and falling back in her chair in a mock swoon. "Ain't it grand!"

Megan threw her hands in the air. "Oh, I give up."

Mollie and Maribeth immediately began clapping and cheering until all three burst into hearty laughter.

"Sounds like you're having a party in here and forgot to invite me," Travis said from the doorway. All three looked around. Danny saw his daddy and immediately started squealing and trying to crawl out of the playpen. Travis reached over and hauled the tot into his arms and began to nuzzle his neck, much to Danny's delight.

Megan scrambled to her feet. "You aren't supposed to be in here! There are things you aren't supposed to see until Christmas."

Mollie had already wrapped most of the gifts Megan had bought for him, but she carefully covered what was still unwrapped that she and Maribeth had found, a routine they'd fallen into years ago since Megan had no patience for making fancy bows and neatly folded corners. She'd only been there today to give them moral support.

Megan slipped her arms beneath Travis's heavy coat and hugged him despite the fact he had his arms full. The gesture was so familiar the sisters thought nothing of it. Travis stepped back long enough to put Danny into his enclosure, then wrapped his arms around her, resting his chin on her head, and looking like a very contented man.

Mollie had a sudden pang of envy at the closeness they shared. Would she ever be able to share a moment like that with Deke? Would she ever dare be so familiar with him?

"So, what was going on in here a while ago?" he repeated, smoothing his hands along Megan's spine. "I heard your voices clear outside."

Maribeth laughed and nodded her head toward the other two women. "That was just Megan shouting at Mollie again."

"My mild-mannered wife raise her soft voice to yell at someone? Why... *ouch*... that doesn't sound like... *ouch*... my sweet— Ow! Stop pinching me!— wife."

"Then stop making fun of me," she replied in her sweetest tone.

"Hey, that's my most favorite thing to do in all the world, woman! Always has been, always will be. Now, stop changing the subject. What's got you gals going in here?"

Megan sighed and reluctantly stepped back from her husband. "Mollie has just announced that she intends to marry Deke Crandall right after Christmas."

"What?" Travis bellowed. The three sisters immediately began laughing all over again. "You can't be serious! Why, you can't possibly— You don't even know— Mollie, that's the most—" He looked at the three of them for a moment, then grinned sheepishly. "That's why you were yelling, right?"

Megan nodded her head, still laughing at his predictable reaction.

"Well, hell. I don't blame you." He strode over to where Mollie was sitting. "How long has this been going on? Have you been seeing him since last summer?"

Then, as though suddenly struck by a thought, his face darkened. "Mollie," he began in a menacing voice, "you aren't—"

"Don't even say it, Travis." Mollie interrupted, hastily coming to her feet. "There's no reason to play the outraged father here. Deke has always been a perfect gentleman with me."

"Speaking of fathers, he's old enough to be—"

"Watch it, Travis! I'm warning you. I don't want to hear any cracks about Deke's age, do you hear me?"

"All I'm saying is—"

"I don't want you saying anything...except whether or not you'd be willing to give me away."

That stopped him cold. He stood there looking at her, blinking in surprise. Then he swallowed. Hard. "You're really serious about this, aren't you?"

She looked him in the eye. "Yes. I really am."

He staggered back and fell on the couch, groaning. "Megan, our chick is trying to fly from the nest. What are we going to do?"

"Honey, I'm afraid she's already flown. She doesn't intend to go back to school. She's going to become a wife and mother in a matter of days."

Travis's head jerked up for a moment, then remembered. "Oh, yeah, that's right." He straightened. "Is it because of the baby, Mollie? I know you got real attached to her last summer, but—"

She held up her hand. "Travis. I will tell you just as I told Megan. I am doing what I want to do and no one is going to stop me. I am twenty years old. I don't need anybody's permission to get married. This is what I want. Just be happy for me, okay?''

Shaking his head, he gave a weary and very disgusted sigh. ''Stubbornness seems to run in the O'Brien family,'' he offered to the room at large, then ducked as three women launched themselves at him in full attack.

Chapter Seven

Today was her wedding day. Mollie was having more than a little trouble accepting the fact that the day had arrived so quickly.

Where had all the time gone? There was so much she'd intended to do, so many things she'd wanted to say—to her family, to Deke. Why, she hadn't even seen Jolene. How was it possible that she was only a few minutes away from repeating vows to a man she hadn't seen since their breakfast together in Austin almost two weeks ago?

At least she had these few minutes alone. Megan had darted out of the small room at the church where Mollie had changed into her wedding gown, looking for Travis. She also wanted to make sure that Deke had actually arrived.

Mollie knew that Megan was hoping he'd had a change of heart. Mollie knew better. She'd spoken to Deke last night. He'd called to see how she was doing, and if she'd gotten all of her packing done and to let her know how much he appreciated what she was doing for him.

She'd been touched by his concern. He'd called her each day since she'd been home. Once he'd suggested that he come over, but she had hastily explained that she was too busy, what with making slight alterations to the wedding gown, which she didn't want him to see, and going through a lifetime accumulation of belongings, wondering what to pitch and what to keep.

What had been more important to her, though, was that she kept Deke and her family as far apart as possible before the ceremony. There was no reason to let Megan and Travis offer their opinions to Deke about the marriage. Of course he'd asked her, but she'd laughingly pointed out how no family is ready to let go of younger siblings. No doubt he knew they weren't pleased and why, but he'd accepted her explanation without comment.

And now, here she stood before the mirror staring at the image of a calm-faced bride, surprised that her nervousness didn't show.

Having the wedding so quickly had had the effect of keeping everyone too busy to try to change her mind.

Mollie had discovered that the only time between Christmas and New Year's the church chapel would be available was Wednesday morning at ten o'clock. The wedding was small, only their closest friends were told about it, and no reception was planned. Megan had taken care of the arrangements at the church, Maribeth and her friends had prepared flowers and candles to be used as decorations, while Mollie sorted through her belongings, getting ready to move away from the O'Brien ranch.

Megan had never had to do that. She still lived in the same house where she'd been born. It was tougher than Mollie had thought it would be...to know that she would be leaving the ranch for good, instead of for just another school term.

Mollie heard a soft tap at the door and Maribeth's voice, saying, "Mollie, it's me."

"Come in," Mollie replied, carefully adjusting a fold in her skirt.

Maribeth slipped in and closed the door. "Oh, Mollie, you look absolutely beautiful."

Mollie grinned. "All brides are beautiful, didn't you know that?"

Maribeth sank into one of the chairs. "I suppose," she said wistfully. Folding her arms, she added, "I don't care what Megan says, I think this is so romantic."

Mollie glanced into the mirror and looked at her sister. Although there was only two years' difference in their ages, Mollie felt years older than Maribeth. It really wasn't Maribeth's fault that both Mollie and Megan had worked hard to protect her from the harsher realities of their orphaned lives. She'd been the baby, only eight when they'd lost their parents. It wasn't that she was spoiled. Maribeth wasn't the type of person who asked for much out of life. She enjoyed her friends, was involved in school activities and was totally oblivious to her startling good looks and her effect on the entire male population. She'd been a tomboy all her life. There was nothing she'd rather do than to hang around with the 4-H group or practice roping and riding with the boys.

Megan had bought Maribeth a dress the soft color of her golden eyes to wear to the wedding. Mollie had gathered her flaming red hair into a cascade of curls at the crown of her head. Maribeth had no idea how stunning she looked, nor did she care.

Mollie smiled at the expression on Maribeth's face. "Are you looking forward to the day you wear this dress?" she asked, more than a little curious about her sister's dreams and fantasies.

"Sure. I mean—" Maribeth shrugged slightly. "I guess I am . . . when the time comes. Bobby and I want to finish college first, but after that, I guess it will be fun to get all dressed up and have a big reception and all the things that go with it. Aren't you a little sad not to have waited to have a big wedding?"

"Not at all. I've never wanted anything like that." She eyed her sister thoughtfully for a moment, then turned away from the mirror. She walked over to where Maribeth sat. "Have you ever had any doubt about wanting to marry Bobby?"

Maribeth laughed. "Of course not. I've always known that someday we'd get married, from as far back as I can remember."

"You've never been interested in any other male at all?"

"Are you kidding? Most guys act so dopey... stuttering and stammering and saying crazy things—like comparing the color of my hair to the sunset, really stupid things like that, or wondering if I wear contacts to make my eyes sparkle. I can't believe they can act so dumb."

"Does Bobby ever pay you compliments?"

Maribeth looked up at her in surprise. "Well, yeah, of course he does. He always brags about me when I do a good job riding or roping. Don't you remember how excited he was for me when I won the barrel race at the county fair rodeo? He's real proud of me."

Mollie grinned and gave her head a tiny shake. "Sounds like true love, all right."

"Why do you ask? Doesn't Deke pay you lots of compliments?"

Mollie was determined not to chuckle at the idea of Deke saying anything more personal to her than complimenting her coffee and biscuits. "Oh, he has his moments," she replied lightly.

"You know, Mollie, Megan's still upset that you wouldn't at least wait until summer to get married. I mean, if he loves you enough, he'd wait for you to at least finish another year of school. I can't believe you wouldn't want to get your degree, though. But then you'd have to wait almost two years, I guess."

Mollie looked into Maribeth's concerned eyes. "I know, but it can't be helped."

"Your getting married now or her being upset?"

"Both," Mollie admitted with a sigh.

There was another tap on the door.

"Come in, Megan," Mollie said, facing the door.

Megan stepped inside, holding Danny in her arms. "Deke's here. He and the pastor are waiting in the chapel, so I guess it's okay for you to come out now."

"Is Mrs. Hobson here to play the organ?"

"I think she's in the church office."

"Okay. As soon as she's ready, have her start playing the prelude we picked and I'll come out. Is Travis handy?"

"He's waiting at the door to the chapel."

Mollie took a deep breath, then smiled at both her sisters. "Okay, here we go. Wish me luck."

Megan slipped her free arm around Mollie and hugged her. "You look just beautiful. I wish you would have let us have the photographer come take pictures."

"I don't think Deke would have been comfortable making a big deal over this."

"Well, that's just too bad. Just because Deke's already gone through all this once doesn't mean—"

"I didn't mean that. And he didn't go through anything like this before. They were married at the courthouse."

"Oh."

"I just know that he's not all that comfortable about having the church wedding and knowing you guys are disturbed about the suddenness of our plans. I didn't see any reason to make things any more tense than they already are."

"Well, I brought my camera. Would you mind if I take some pictures after the ceremony?" Megan asked.

"I'd love to have them," Mollie admitted.

Maribeth stood and came over to them. "Go find Mrs. Hobson so we can get this show on the road, okay?" she said to Megan. Glancing down at her dress, she added, "I can hardly wait to change back into my jeans. I feel half naked in this thing."

"You've got beautiful legs, Maribeth. You should enjoy showing them off," Mollie said.

Maribeth glanced down in surprise. "I do?"

"Yes, you do," Megan replied. "They're very shapely."

She frowned. "So? Legs are legs, aren't they?"

Mollie and Megan shared a glance and a smile. "I'll see you in a few minutes," Megan said, giving a quick squeeze to Mollie's hand and slipping out the door.

Maribeth adjusted the short veil around Mollie's face. "You look so calm."

"I'm glad. I don't want Deke to think I have any concerns about marrying him." And of course she didn't. Not really. But her whole life was going to change as soon as she stepped out of this room. It would never be the same again.

* * *

Deke couldn't believe that he was standing there in front of these people wearing a formal suit and tie. He never wore ties. But this was what Mollie had wanted and he couldn't say no.

He stood next to the pastor, a man he'd known for years, and watched the doorway for Mollie and Travis to appear.

He'd felt a definite frost in the air from the family when he'd showed up this morning. They'd probably been hoping he'd changed his mind. Mollie had already told him about their reaction and he couldn't blame them.

He saw a shadowy movement at the back of the chapel and the organist immediately changed the quiet background music to the familiar strains of the wedding march.

His heart felt as though it was in his throat. He tugged at the collar of his shirt and tried to swallow. There she was, dressed in a long gown that revealed her small waist and curving breasts and hips. A short veil hid her expression from him. He fought not to show how uncomfortable he was in this setting. Thank God there were only a few people there to watch them.

Then she was standing beside him and he looked at the pastor for direction.

Soon the words of the traditional ceremony flowed over him—soothing, compassionate, a blessing for the future, much more loving than the terse words once said to him at the courthouse.

He learned that Mollie's real name was Mary Katherine, while she and everybody there learned that his real name was Dewayne Kenneth, an embarrassment for him his entire life.

Travis spoke up in his firm voice to give her away and diplomatically remained silent when the question was asked if anyone objected. Before Deke knew it, he was putting a ring on Mollie's finger, a gold band that he had purchased in Austin the day she'd agreed to marry him.

It was time for him to kiss the bride. How strange to realize only in that moment that he had never kissed her, but then, there had been good reason for not doing so. It would have been out of place and unconscionable to have shown a personal interest in her last summer, and their visits together in Austin had been more like a business deal than a romantic date.

Regardless of how it had been arranged, the fact was that Mollie O'Brien Crandall was now his lawfully wedded wife.

He could feel his blood racing. He reached over to lift her veil and noted that his fingers trembled slightly. When he folded the netting back over her head, he met her gaze and his heart thundered in his chest. She looked up at him with eyes filled with so much trust. Never had she looked at him with that kind of warmth and—could it possibly be?—affection.

Carefully he brushed his lips against hers, feeling them quiver. For a brief time he allowed his mouth to linger on hers, reassured by the contact and the slight return of pressure. At least she hadn't flinched or drawn away from him.

Slowly he straightened, still holding her hands clasped in his. Only then did the organ burst forth with a fanfare of chords. The people attending the service all stood when the pastor turned the couple to the gathering and introduced them for the first time as Mr. and Mrs. Crandall.

A flash suddenly went off nearby and he glanced at the front row where Megan stood, snapping pictures. Maribeth held Danny while Travis and several friends came toward them, laughing and wishing them well.

Thank God it was over! was all he could think as the visitors shook his hand and kissed Mollie on the cheek. It was the most natural thing in the world for him to slip his arm around her waist, cupping his hand over her hip.

Was it his imagination or did she lean slightly into him? He glanced down at her but she was listening to one of the women who had taken care of Jolene last summer.

Thankfully people had other places to go and things to do, and Deke heard himself talking about getting everyone together for a party at the ranch once the weather warmed up. He'd never done anything like that before, but the more he thought about, the better he liked the idea.

After everyone but the family had gone, Travis drew Deke aside.

"I wanted to do something for the two of you to help get this marriage off in a traditional way," Travis said to him in a low voice, "so I've made reservations for you and Mollie to stay at one of those fancy hotels along the river in San Antonio for the next two nights, all expenses paid. I figured y'all could use some time together away from the ranch and the baby."

Deke was dumbfounded. He couldn't think of anything to say. How could he explain that he and Mollie wouldn't be sharing a room in the foreseeable future? Mollie turned toward them and Deke realized that she had heard Travis. Her face was rosy.

"Oh, Travis, you didn't have to do that!" she said, and Deke wanted to add his agreement but couldn't seem to find the right words.

Travis shrugged. "It's my wedding present to y'all. You didn't give us much of a chance to do anything more."

Mollie looked at Deke, obviously waiting for him to deal with this latest situation. What could he say, after all?

"That's mighty nice of you, Travis," he murmured, shaking hands with his new brother-in-law. "I really appreciate the gesture." Once again he dropped his arm casually around Mollie's waist and gave her a gentle squeeze. "Sounds kinda fun, doesn't it, honey?" he asked, causing her to blink at him in surprise.

Her bright color and stammering response could be taken for a new bride's shyness.

Travis smiled at Mollie and winked at Deke. "Looks like you have a blushing bride, all right. Guess it's part of the tradition, after all. I just wanted to say that while you're gone, I'll see that all of Mollie's things get out to your place. Megan and I will make sure Mrs. Franzke doesn't need anything. If she does, she can always give us a call."

Deke glanced down at Mollie and wasn't surprised to discover that she wouldn't meet his gaze. "I don't know about you, honey," he drawled, "but I'd be much more comfortable if I could change into something else before we head down to San Antonio. How about you?"

"Oh! Yes, of course. I wouldn't want to wear this. I'm afraid it's a little too conspicuous." She motioned toward the back of the church. "I brought something to change into. Did you?"

"Guess I wasn't that prepared. But once you've changed, we can run out to the ranch, tell Mrs. Franzke our plans and let you see Jolene while I change clothes. That sound all right with you?"

She nodded, then turned away. For a moment he wanted to follow her, to ask her what she wanted to do, but this wasn't the time, so he watched as she retreated up the aisle, her sisters following her. Travis now held Danny who was showing signs of restlessness.

"They sure grow up quick, don't they?" Travis said, finally allowing the toddler down and firmly holding his tiny hand. "He's gotten to be quite a handful since he's been walking. We have to watch him every second."

Deke looked at the baby. He was a sturdy little boy, nothing babyish about him, with his dad's dark good looks. Deke swallowed and looked away.

"Is Jolene walking?"

"Uh, yeah, she's beginning to."

"We'll have to let them play together once they're a little older. Megan and I want a large family. We're already talking about our next one," he said with a grin.

Deke wanted no part of this conversation. "I'll go check on Mollie to see if she's changed," he managed to say. "Thanks again for the trip. I hadn't given much thought to what we'd do after the ceremony. I guess I just assumed—" He stopped, not wanting to get into that particular subject, either. He shrugged and headed toward the back of the chapel.

He was standing in the church foyer when he caught movement out of the corner of his eye. He turned and saw Mollie coming toward him. She wore a blue, heavy knit sweater and a matching blue plaid woolen skirt and blue high heels. She looked stunning. Blue was definitely her color. He'd never noticed her legs before, and fought to control the impact she'd made on him. "I'm ready whenever you are," she said, not quite meeting his eyes.

"Then let's get out of here," he growled, grabbing her hand. He heard Travis chuckle behind him. Megan and Maribeth had followed her from the dressing room, carrying her wedding gown and veil.

"Give us a call when you get back," Megan said, her voice wobbling.

Maribeth grinned. "They aren't flying around the world, you know."

Mollie laughed and turned back to give each of them a quick hug. "Thank you for everything. I couldn't have put this together without you. I love you so much."

"Now don't start that," Megan said. "I was determined not to cry, darn it!" She grabbed her purse and started searching for a handkerchief.

Deke added his thanks to everyone, then took Mollie's hand and led her outside to his truck. "Hope you don't mind me rushing you, but I've got to get out of these clothes," he said, pulling off his tie. "I can't understand why anybody would want to wear them."

"It's okay. I'll see them again in a few days. Wasn't it sweet of Travis to offer to get my things over to your place for me?"

"I don't know that I'd call it sweet, exactly, but it was a thoughtful gesture. I should have thought of that. Guess I haven't been thinking too clearly this week. I never gave a thought to our going off anywhere. I guess I was planning to bring you home and put you to work immediately," he said in disgust.

"Don't feel bad... that's what I thought was going to happen, too. When is Mrs. Franzke leaving?"

"Oh, she said she could stay a couple more weeks if I needed her, so there isn't a problem with that." He glanced at Mollie out of the corner of his eye. "I just wasn't thinking about a honeymoon, that's all."

Mollie folded her hands in her lap and looked straight ahead. "Honeymoons are part of the tradition."

"Well, sure, if it's a real wedding and all."

Next she trained her gaze on her clasped hands. "Ours was a real wedding, Deke."

"You know what I mean."

Mollie didn't say anything more and darn if he could think of anything to break the silence. Why was it that he felt he had done or said something wrong? Didn't they have an understanding, after all? They were married, but not really. She would be staying in her room and he would be staying in—

Damn. He'd forgotten. She wouldn't have a room as long as Mrs. Franzke was there. He turned off the highway onto the ranch road, already feeling the beginnings of a headache. There were several things he hadn't thought through, obviously. Somehow, they'd get through these next few weeks. It was just that, at the moment, he wasn't certain how.

Mrs. Franzke greeted them as soon as they walked through the door. "Oh, there you are! I tried to keep Jolene awake but she was so fussy I finally fed her and put her down for her nap." She smiled at Mollie. "You must be eager to see her again."

"Oh, I am! I'll just peek in on her," she said, heading down the hallway.

Deke pulled off his suit coat and started down the hall, then paused and turned to Mrs. Franzke. "Mollie's brother-in-law has arranged for us to spend the next couple of nights in San Antonio. He said they would be available if there's an emergency of any kind."

Mrs. Franzke smiled. "What a lovely thing for him to do. You and Mollie will enjoy some time alone, I'm sure."

He wanted to argue that point, but knew better. "Yeah, right. I, uh, thought I'd change clothes and, uh, pack a few things to take with me."

"You're a very lucky man, Deke, to get such a loving woman as Mollie. She's going to make a wonderful mother for little Jolene."

His guilt gnawed at him. "I know," he muttered and escaped down the hallway. He paused at the door to Jolene's room and watched Mollie as she carefully rearranged the covers over the baby. Her tender smile caused a lump in his throat. He moved away, thoughtfully going into his room to get ready for his wedding trip.

He knew he was way over his head on this one, but there wasn't a thing he could think of to do about it at this point. Somehow, he had to believe that everything would work out all right for the three of them.

However, it was definitely a long shot in his book.

Chapter Eight

The winter sun had already disappeared by the time they reached San Antonio that evening. Mollie could feel the beginnings of a headache coming on, no doubt due to the strain of the past two hours—the length of the drive from Agua Verde to San Antonio.

She'd tried to make conversation but Deke was obviously distracted. He showed no interest in any of her casual comments so that eventually she gave up trying to get him to talk. With a hint of desperation, she turned on the radio, wondering if he was upset because Travis had arranged this trip.

She was glad they had come. After all, this was her wedding, the only one she would ever have, no matter what she had teased Deke with when they'd first discussed the possibility. For some reason she had thought that Deke would be more relaxed after the ceremony was behind them. Wasn't this what he'd wanted? It wasn't as though she'd come up with the idea and forced it on him.

Perhaps he was being reminded of his first marriage, comparing the two, and finding Mollie considerably less appealing than he'd first thought.

Well, if that was the case, then she would have to show him that he hadn't made a mistake in choosing to marry Mollie O'Brien. She was determined to make him a good wife and Jolene a loving mother.

They found the hotel with no trouble. It towered above the surrounding buildings. Mollie couldn't help but be impressed. She'd never stayed in a hotel before, of any kind. She was pleased that her first experience would be in luxurious surroundings.

Deke found a parking space and pulled in. He turned off the engine and lights, then turned to face her. "Mollie—" he began, then stopped.

"Yes?"

"Maybe this wasn't such a good idea, after all."

She waited for him to continue. When he didn't, she probed with a question. "Are you talking about our marriage or coming to San Antonio?"

Her question seemed to disconcert him and he gave her a lopsided grin as he reached for her hand. Folding it into his much larger one, he said, "Both, probably, but I was talking about staying here." He nodded his head toward the entrance to the hotel.

She glanced in the same direction. "Why? It looks quite nice."

He leaned his shoulder against the door of the truck, then carefully laced his fingers between hers. She found the handclasp surprisingly intimate. The warmth of his fingers surrounded hers, and the palm of his callused hand caused hers to tingle.

"When I was considering all the reasons for getting married and how we might make it work, I kept seeing us at the ranch, much as we were last summer—you looking after Jolene and me working outside. I figured that I could stay at the house this time, since there was no need to worry about your reputation, but the thing is, I never gave a thought to the possibility of us sharing a room."

"Oh."

"Yeah. Oh. It hit me this afternoon that until Mrs. Franzke leaves, your room won't be available. Now, here we are ready to check into the hotel as Mr. and Mrs. and we'll be expected to share a room."

Somehow his voice seemed to have dropped a couple of notches during his explanation. The tingling that had begun in her palm was now running up her arm until she felt it all through her body. She shifted slightly, her knee coming to rest against his thigh.

"Well," she finally said, feeling a bit breathless, "I guess that's fairly normal for married people, isn't it?"

"Sure, if this was a normal marriage."

"But you don't want a real marriage."

He muttered something under his breath, then raised their clasped hands and brushed his mouth against her knuckles. "I never said that."

Her body seemed to be vibrating to some silent tune playing around them. "Uh, does that mean that you *do* want us to have a—uh—" She couldn't quite find the words to use and stumbled to a halt.

Deke nibbled on her knuckles, then gently soothed them with his tongue. "It doesn't matter what I want," he said. "You're the one calling the shots here."

She straightened in surprise. "I am?"

His chuckle sounded a little pained. "Oh, yes. There's no doubt about that. From planning the wedding to when and where it would take place, to—"

"But I only wanted—"

"I know," he said soothingly, "I wanted you to be happy with the arrangements. I still do. So I'm willing to play this out any way you want."

A bubble of excitement seemed to grow in her chest. Deke was offering her choices. He was willing to accept whatever she decided. So now all she had to figure out was what she wanted.

That didn't take much thought.

"Then could we get something to eat?" she asked. "I'm starving."

He stared at her in disbelief. "You're hungry?" he drawled, as though never having heard of the condition.

"Aren't you? We skipped lunch, you know. I thought about saying something once we got on the road, but then I thought... Well, you seemed so quiet and I didn't want to—''

Deke began to laugh, a hearty sound she had not heard from him since the day she first saw him many years ago. She couldn't believe the change it made in him. He looked years younger, and actually happy. She soon joined him.

"I guess I'm not being very romantic, am I?" she finally asked.

"But oh, so very practical." He pulled her into his arms and gave her a hug. "God, I'm lucky you came into my life. I can't believe how lucky."

She tucked her face into his shoulder for a moment, loving the feel of his arms around her, before she leaned back so that she could once again see his face. His eyes were dancing and his smile flashed bright in the darkened cab of the truck. "You didn't seem all that thrilled when you finally came to the door," she reminded him.

"True. I should have known then that you're used to getting your own way."

Before she could do more than sputter, Deke opened the door and stepped out of the truck. "C'mon, woman, let's go find you some food before you start looking for something else to sink your teeth into."

His grin and the heat in his eyes made her blush, even if she wasn't certain exactly why he looked so amused.

Deke found their reservations waiting at the desk. He also inquired about the restaurant that they could see through wide doors off the lobby and was told they could go eat while their luggage was sent up to their room.

Deke took her hand and escorted her into the dimly lit restaurant. There was a small musical combo playing and a few people were dancing. He glanced down at her.

"Do you like to dance?"

"Yes, but I've never danced anywhere but at school functions."

"Let's get you fed, then maybe we can do a couple of turns around the floor. What do you say?"

She knew her heart must be in her eyes when she replied, "I'd like that...very much." All at once all the dreams and fantasies of her childhood had leaped into being, but this was even better than a child's wild imaginings. This was real. She was here with Deke Crandall and she was his wife. A dream come true.

Deke had definitely gone through an abrupt mood change since they'd left Agua Verde. After communicating in monosyllables during the drive down, he was now keeping the conversation going by asking her all kinds of questions. Unfortunately they were about her, a subject that couldn't be more boring.

"You actually took over the cooking when you were ten?" he was saying, his voice echoing his amazement, his eyes as he watched her still warm and glowing.

"They certainly weren't gourmet meals, if that's what you're thinking. You have to remember that I was always fascinated watching my mother in the kitchen, until she finally put me to work. She showed me how to measure, how to follow simple recipes. I found it all great fun. Lots of little girls play at cooking. I was lucky enough that my mother was willing to let me use real ingredients.''

"Was Megan interested in all of that?''

Mollie chuckled. "Hardly. No, Megan has always been the one who followed Dad everywhere. She was probably riding a horse by the time she could walk. Remember she was a few years older than me, so we didn't have much in common.''

"But you got along?''

"Sure. Probably because we were so different. I admired her skills that were honed working the ranch, knowing I could never do any of it. She seemed to admire what I did around the house, even though she claimed not to have any patience for it.'' Mollie grinned. "Of course, now that Danny's here, her domestic side is certainly showing up. She dotes on him.''

"Travis mentioned that they're already talking about having more.''

"Now that's news! She hasn't mentioned it to me. How did he happen to say something to you?''

Deke shifted uncomfortably in his chair. "Ah—well, I'm not really sure, now that you mention it. I think he said something about how fast babies grow up.''

"Oh, yes, that's true. I should be getting used to it after seeing how much Danny changed while I was away from home, but when I saw Jolene I was still amazed at how much she's changed.'' She glanced around the softly lit room. "I'm not sorry to get to see and experience all of this, but I can't wait to get back to see Jolene, to get her used to having me around, you know what I mean?''

Deke's smile faded. "Yes."

"Deke?"

"Yes?"

"Why don't you show more interest in Jolene? I know it was really hard on you at first, and you probably blamed—"

"Look, Mollie, I don't want to talk about Jolene, okay? I think it's great that you love her and were willing to commit to marrying me in order to care for her. But I don't want to discuss her with you."

The formidable expression had reappeared and Mollie felt totally lost. What had happened? They had been having a lighthearted conversation just minutes ago, and then— Ah. The conversation had been about her and her family. He could handle that. But any reminders of his life, which would include Jolene, was obviously off limits.

Mollie fought to hide her disappointment at his rapid mood change. The fast rhythm of the band came to an end and they immediately shifted into another song, this time a slow blues number.

On impulse, Mollie asked, "Are you ready to dance with me?"

Deke glanced at the dance floor where several couples were circling, then back to her. "Sure. Why not?" He rose and pulled her chair out for her, then guided her to the dance floor. Once there, Mollie turned and waited for him to take her into his arms.

She certainly wasn't disappointed now. With practiced skill Deke slipped his arm around her waist and snuggled her to his body. He took her hand and clasped it against his shoulder, then looked at her with an unreadable expression. "This may not have been such a good idea, after all," he murmured.

Mollie had never been so close to anyone before. She tentatively placed her other hand on his shoulder, glad that she was wearing high heels. His lips rested against her forehead and she could feel his warm breath, not to mention the hard, muscled length of his body.

"What's wrong?" she managed to whisper, suddenly feeling very unlike herself. Her breasts were pressed against his chest and they had become unbearably sensitive to every subtle shift of his body.

The movement of his thighs guided hers in the agonizingly slow pace of the song being played.

"Let's just say that I'm glad it's fairly dark in here, otherwise we might both be embarrassed."

Only then did Mollie realize what he must be referring to, and she could feel her face burning. It wasn't as if she didn't know and understand all about human anatomy and the difference between the genders. It was just that this was the first time she'd had a physical demonstration of the phenomenon. Despite her embarrassment, Mollie felt a surge of excitement. Holding her this close, Deke couldn't hide his response to her. He wanted her, at least on the most basic level, but it was enough at the moment to make her feel ready to take the next step.

Deke wasn't ready to share his life and his heart with her. She could only hope that once he accepted their new relationship that he would someday open up to her.

In the meantime, she was going to do whatever she could to show him that she loved him unconditionally.

Deke edged away from her in a turn and she unobtrusively stepped closer.

"Mollie—" His voice held a definite warning.

"Mmm?" She'd closed her eyes to better savor the sensation of being so close to him.

"The trouble with playing with fire, honey, is that sometimes you can get burned."

She went up on tiptoes and kissed his ear. "Really? But sometimes the beauty of the flames is worth it, don't you think?"

Before he could reply, the song ended to a polite patter of applause. "C'mon," he said gruffly, "let's get out of here."

Since he was leading her off the dance floor toward their table, he didn't see her delighted grin. Pausing only long enough to sign their dinner tab, he led her to the bank of elevators without looking at her.

The elevator was crowded and he placed her directly in front of him. She deliberately leaned back against him, shifting her weight so that her bottom rubbed enticingly across him. She heard a hiss of air being drawn between clenched teeth and smiled to herself.

Once they reached their floor, Deke wasted no time striding down the hallway until he located their room. He opened the door and motioned for her to enter. He wouldn't meet her eyes.

A lamp glowed across the room by the sliding doors that led out onto a balcony. The drapes were open and drew Mollie's attention to the view. Deke disappeared into the bathroom, firmly closing the door behind him and leaving her alone.

The room was large, which was a good thing, since the mammoth bed took up so much space. There was also a love seat and a round table with two comfortable-looking chairs.

Mollie opened the sliding glass door and stepped out onto the balcony. The city lights twinkled back at her. Down below the winding river made its picturesque way through the heart of the city.

She heard the bathroom door open and without looking around she said, "Oh, Deke, come look at the view. I can't believe it's so beautiful."

She could feel his presence even though he didn't say anything when he first stepped outside. They stood in silence for several minutes before he spoke. "Yes," he said in a low voice. "Very beautiful."

When she glanced around she saw that he wasn't looking at the view. His gaze was fixed on her. She straightened from where she'd been leaning on the railing and slowly turned to face him.

"Deke?" she whispered.

He edged her back until she was pressed against the smooth siding of the building, then placed his forearms on either side of her head. "You're driving me crazy. You know that, don't you?" he replied, but didn't give her time to respond before he captured her mouth in an explosive, mind-numbing kiss.

He allowed his long length to rest against her, not hard enough to be heavy, but to make her fully aware of him and his present condition. Then he deliberately shifted so that he rubbed against her.

The effect on her was electrifying. A bolt of excitement shot through her, making her groan with pleasure, and she wrapped her arms tightly around his neck.

He leisurely explored the shape of her mouth with his tongue, stroking lightly, then nipping at her bottom lip. When she couldn't hold back a slight gasp, he took advantage of her parted lips and took his exploration deeper.

Mollie's knees refused to bear her weight and she sagged against him. Without releasing her mouth, he swept her up into his arms and carried her back into the bedroom.

He finally lifted his head and stared down at her, breathing hard. "I hope...you haven't just been... teasing me...to see if...you could get a...reaction," he said. "'Cause you may get more than you... bargained for." He leaned his knee on the bed and lowered her to its surface, following her down and leaning over her, his breath still coming unevenly.

Mollie felt as if she was floating. She'd never experienced anything resembling what he was making her feel now. And she wanted more. So much more, even if she didn't know what it was that she wanted. Mostly she didn't want him to stop. . . for any reason.

With her eyes still closed, Mollie urged his mouth back down to meet hers. She felt—more than heard—a brief chuckle as, once again, he allowed her to have her way.

She tugged at the buttons of his Western shirt, glad that they snapped and so quickly responded to her efforts. With fevered longing she touched his bare chest, her fingertips sensitized to the feel of soft hair snugly curling around them.

Deke kept his weight off her by leaning on his forearms, which pressed their lower bodies together more tightly. She shifted, moving her legs so that one of his knees slipped between hers. He groaned when she clamped her legs around him.

Mollie had no idea what she was doing and she didn't care. Nothing she and Deke could do together could be wrong. She loved him. Of course she did, or she would never have married him. Someday maybe she'd be able to tell him that. Until then, she would show him how she felt.

Deke sat up, leaning on his haunches. "You've got entirely too many clothes on," he said, his eyes heated pools of emotion. He reached for her sweater and she obligingly lifted until he could tug it over her head. Tossing the garment aside, he reached behind her and unsnapped her bra. Drawing it slowly away from her, he stared down at her breasts with unfeigned pleasure.

"Oh, Mollie, you are even more beautiful than I could possibly have imagined."

Mollie was surprised to discover the pleasure his words gave her. Even more surprised was she to realize she wasn't embarrassed at having him look at her. She was shyly pleased that he found her attractive, grateful to know that perhaps she could give him pleasure, too.

He unfastened her skirt and slid it, together with her slip and panty hose, down her legs, removing her shoes and tossing the bundle to join her sweater. Only her scrap of lace panties remained.

"How about you? Aren't you going to—" She motioned, calling his attention to the fact that he still wore his boots and jeans, his shirt hanging on his shoulders.

He shook his head as he rolled over and tugged on his boots. "You make me crazy. I can't even think," he muttered as though to himself.

Within moments he'd stripped to his briefs, then he paused to pull the covers back. Scooping her into his arms he held her close to his chest for a long moment, looking down at her in wonderment.

"Do you have any idea how beautiful you are?"

"I'm glad you think so."

"But you don't agree."

"I'm average looking, I guess."

He just shook his head and lowered them both to the smooth expanse of sheets. "I'm not sure what it's gonna take to convince you, but I'm sure gonna try."

He touched her as though she were a priceless, fragile piece of artwork to be gently stroked and fondled, but never handled roughly.

Everywhere his fingers trailed, her skin tingled and leaped into a new awareness. She'd had no idea her body had so many sensitive spots. With his tongue he stroked the hollow at the base of her throat, causing her to shiver. He ran his fingertips in a circle around her breasts, moving them in an ever smaller circle until they paused on the quivering tips, hardened with arousal.

He followed the contour of her ribs down to her waist, then leaned over and kissed her belly button, tracing it with his tongue. By the time his fingers slipped beneath the lacy edge of her panties, Mollie felt like a trembling mass of nerve ends, all screaming for a release she knew nothing about.

He took her hand and gently guided her to touch him. Her eyes widened—as she tentatively followed the hardened length—to feel him quiver.

"I don't want this to hurt you," he said, beads of moisture across his brow. "I've never— It's been so— Oh, honey. I want this to be good for you." His fingers continued to explore beneath the only piece of clothing she still wore.

Only then did she discover that she was moist and so hot there. His fingers felt wonderful to her, as though he knew what she needed, what she had to have. Reflexively she lifted her hips to him, encouraging him in the only way she knew, not to stop.

The lamp created an aureole of golden light around him, touching his blond hair, burnishing his deep tan, and she could only marvel at his masculine beauty. Only as an adult could she fully appreciate all this man was. The reality of the man far surpassed any childhood memories that might have lingered.

Deke slipped off the remaining barriers between them and knelt over her, still loving her with his hands and mouth. Too impatient to wait for him, she wrapped her arms and legs around him and clung to him, making him laugh aloud at her eagerness.

Glorious moments later she was rewarded as he slowly and carefully took possession of her. She was so aroused that she scarcely noticed the momentary barrier and could only sigh when he was fully seated deep within her.

"Oh, Mollie, honey, you feel so good. Oh baby, I can't believe how good you feel to me." He held her as tightly as she was holding him while he continued to place hot kisses along her brow, nose, cheek, jaw and finally settled on her mouth with passionate intent.

Mollie felt surrounded by his loving presence. When he began to move slowly in an achingly provocative movement she met him with an equally arousing lift and thrust, matching him, encouraging him until she lost all sense of place . . . and time . . . and began to experience the most astounding physical responses.

She clung to him, panting for air all the while she clutched him closer and closer until everything seemed to explode around her, inside and out, her body pulsating and throbbing in a rhythm that was new and yet as old as time.

Deke groaned as he made one final lunge before collapsing over her, his hair damp with perspiration, falling across her cheek as he buried his face in her neck.

They lay that way for uncounted minutes before Deke finally shifted slightly. "I'm too heavy," he managed to say.

"Oh, no," she said, unable to contain her emotions so that they overflowed into tears of love and joy. "You're just right. Please don't move."

He shifted a little more, so that most of his weight was on his hip as he slid to one side of her. "I'm not going far, believe me."

She could feel his heart still racing in his chest. She placed her palm over it, loving the strong, solid rhythm of it.

She must have dozed because she awoke sometime later when Deke pulled the covers around them. He must have also turned off the light, since the room was now in darkness. Before she could get her brain working again, he gathered her into his arms and she drifted off once again into a deep, dreamless sleep.

Chapter Nine

Bright sunlight shining in her face woke Mollie the next morning. Since the sun didn't come into her bedroom window either at school or at home, she was disoriented. Where in the world was she?

Then the radiating heat along her back and cupped behind her knees reminded her of not only where she was but with whom.

She couldn't suppress the smile that hovered around her mouth.

They'd gone to bed rather suddenly last night, as she recalled with secret relish, without closing the drapes. She glanced at the clock, amazed to see it was after nine o'clock. She was usually awake hours before this. But if you couldn't sleep in on the morning after you'd gotten married, she reminded herself, then there was nothing fair about this world.

She edged away from Deke and carefully slipped out of bed. He never stirred. She turned back to study him for these few private moments. Thick lashes shadowed his cheeks, which were already showing signs of a needed shave. His tanned shoulders made a strong contrast against the whiteness of the sheets.

Wearing a smile of pure pleasure she reluctantly turned away and headed to the bathroom. Once she was moving she discovered a few little aches that were new to her experiences. So what? She didn't mind when so many other sensations had been so extraordinary.

Mollie let the hot water soothe her body for several minutes before she soaped herself, rinsed, then crawled out of the shower. There were matching robes hanging on the door with the hotel's logo on the pockets. As soon as she'd dried off, she slipped into one of them and reentered the bedroom.

Deke hadn't moved.

Mollie stepped out onto the balcony, enjoying the feel of the warm sunshine after the past several days of cold, blustery winter. She turned her face up to the sun and closed her eyes, luxuriating in the simple, sensual pleasure.

A pair of arms suddenly snaked around her waist and she let out a little squeak. "Deke! You scared me."

He nibbled on her ear. "Really? Who did you think it was?"

"I thought you were asleep."

"I was. Then I woke up. You looked too delicious standing out here to be ignored."

Only then did she realize that he was standing out on the balcony without a stitch of clothing. "Deke! What if somebody sees you like that!"

"Like what?" he asked, all innocence. "You're standing in front of me."

She looked wildly around before relaxing slightly. People from below wouldn't be able to see him, and anyone looking from the buildings across the river would only see his bare shoulders.

She turned in his arms, inadvertently untying the sash of her robe, so that it immediately fell open, leaving her bare skin pressing against his.

"Ah, I must admit that this is even better," he said, his mouth seeking hers while his hands decided to explore.

Her newly tutored body immediately responded with enthusiasm and before long Deke was backing toward the bed while she eagerly followed. The bed caught him behind the knees and he toppled backward, laughing as Mollie tumbled down on top of him.

He wasted no time showing her how much pleasure she could experience while she was in that position.

When she next looked at the clock, it was noon, and they were still in bed.

"Aren't you hungry?" she asked. "We've missed breakfast and it's already time for lunch."

"What can I do about it? I'm being held captive by a love-hungry woman who won't let me out of bed," he drawled. He might have been more convincing if he didn't look so smug.

"Maybe we could order from room service. I noticed there's a full selection. That would be really different, to have someone waiting on us for a change."

He opened one eye. "I think I'd be safer if we got dressed and stayed away from any beds for the next few hours."

"Oh, you," she said, poking him in the ribs and grinning.

"Why don't you take a shower with me?"

She gave him a haughty stare. "Do you dare trust me not to attack you while you're helpless?"

He rolled over and dragged her off the bed with him. "I'm never helpless, woman. Drained and weak, maybe, but—" He began to laugh at her expression. "I can't believe how much fun you are to tease. I may have found a whole new hobby." He led her into the bathroom and turned on the shower. "Maybe tonight we'll try out the tub. Look. It's got air jets, room for two. We could probably spend hours in here."

"True, but you'd have to take your clothes off for that, as well, leaving you vulnerable."

"That works both ways, honey. And I intend to enjoy every minute of our time together...starting now." He stepped into the shower, helping her to join him, then lovingly soaped every inch of her body before magnanimously offering her the soap to do the same thing to him.

They never did manage to leave the room that day and were thankful for room service. Otherwise, they might have starved.

By the time they returned to the ranch, Mollie felt confident that she and Deke had made great strides in their relationship. She couldn't believe how different he'd been with her once he discovered her eagerness to explore and experience the physical side of their union. He'd become a teasing, delightful lover, considerate of her every need.

When they pulled up in front of the ranch house, she felt certain that the awkwardness of their first few hours of marriage was gone for good.

Mrs. Franzke met them at the door. "I don't need to ask how you enjoyed your stay in San Antonio," she offered, beaming. "You both are positively glowing."

"Glowing?" Deke repeated, arching a brow.

Mrs. Franzke laughed. "Close enough." She turned away to pour them some coffee. "Travis brought Mollie's things. I hope you don't mind that I went ahead and put them in your room," she said, looking at Deke. "I had to make room in your closet for a few things, and I used the chest of drawers that was empty."

Mollie responded. "That was kind of you, but I could have unpacked once I got back."

"I know, but I figured you might have your hands full with Jolene. She seems to have picked up a little cold, probably due to the changeable weather. Sometimes it's difficult to know how to dress a little one. I don't think it's anything to be concerned about, but she's been really fussy. I figured until you settled into a routine, you'd probably want to spend most of your time with her, so I put things away whenever I had a spare moment.''

"Where is she?" Mollie asked. "Is she asleep? Maybe I could go check on her.''

"She's in bed, and since I haven't heard anything out of her for the past few minutes, I guess she's still asleep. She'll certainly let you know fast enough when she's awake.''

Mollie hurried into the hallway and down to Jolene's room. The baby was sitting up in bed, rubbing her eyes.

"Well, hello, darlin'. Did you have a nice nap?''

Jolene blinked at her solemnly.

"Do you remember me? Oh, I hope so. You and I used to have so much fun together. Remember that?'' She reached for Jolene, smoothing her hand across her forehead. "Do you have a fever, sugar?'' she wondered, and was relieved to feel the normal warmth radiating from her.

Jolene held up her hands and gave an impatient grunt and bounce.

"Oh, yes, ma'am. You're going to be friendly with anybody who'll pick you up, aren't you? Come on. Let's get you into some dry diapers, then we'll go see your daddy. How's that?''

Jolene stared at her for a moment before she began to babble some kind of language that caused Mollie to laugh. After she'd changed her new little daughter,

Mollie gathered her up and took her back to the kitchen.

"Would you look at— Deke?"

Mrs. Franzke was alone in the kitchen.

"Where's Deke?"

"Said he needed to check with the foreman about what's been going on since he was gone." She smiled at Jolene. "So you remembered Mollie, did you?"

"Either that, or she's willing to make friends quickly. She's really a chunk now, isn't she? How much does she weigh?"

Mrs. Franzke gave her the pertinent statistics and the two of them spent the rest of the day visiting with each other, going over Jolene's routine and helping to get Mollie settled into her new home.

"If you wouldn't be upset," Mrs. Franzke said later that day, "I've been thinking about leaving earlier than I first mentioned to Deke. Of course I'd stay if I thought you really needed me, but it looks like you're already comfortable with the baby and I would like to get over to my sister's in time to help bring her home from the hospital. The doctor is talking about letting her come home in a few days."

"That's fine with me, Mrs. Franzke. I'm sure Deke would understand."

"Well, I'll check with him this evening. I guess I'd better get a meal put together."

"Why don't you sit back and relax now that we're back home? I'd enjoy doing some cooking after all those months at school."

"Aren't you going to miss going to college, my dear?"

Mollie laughed. "Not at all. I couldn't be happier doing what I'm doing right now," she said as she placed Jolene in her high chair.

Her words echoed in her head as she looked through the freezer and pantry to decide what to make for Deke's dinner. She wondered if he understood how important it was for her to see him enjoy her meals, or how good it had made her feel when he commented on the little touches she'd added to his home.

He'd left little doubt in her mind during the past couple of days that he enjoyed her in other ways. In fact, after being in his constant presence for that length of time, she'd found herself missing him as the afternoon wore on.

She knew the ranch was important to him, of course. He hadn't even waited to see Jolene before going out there. But then, he expected her to look after the baby.

Mollie just wished he spent more time with his tiny daughter. She wasn't certain how, but she knew she was going to do everything she could to help him come closer to Jolene.

During the next few weeks, Mollie found herself making the same resolve on more than one occasion and feeling frustrated when Deke reverted to the schedule he'd kept last summer...with one notable exception. He spent each night with her, not out in the bunkhouse.

She couldn't have asked for a more loving, giving husband. He'd willingly driven Mrs. Franzke back to Austin to be with her sister, he'd spent his evenings and nights showing Mollie how much he needed and wanted her, but whenever Jolene was in the room, he found reasons to be somewhere else.

She wasn't imagining it, that was certain. Whenever she attempted to talk to him about the baby, he'd change the subject. Mollie couldn't understand how he could ignore such an adorable, happy child.

One evening while Mollie was trying to get everything on the table, Deke wandered into the kitchen after his shower just as Jolene let out a loud wail from her room, long after she was supposed to be down for the night. Glancing over at the timer, Mollie rushed to the oven, saying, "Would you check on Jolene for me, please? I've got to get this roast out of the oven before it dries out."

"I'll get the roast," he immediately replied. "You can see why she's crying."

Mollie had already opened the oven door by the time he spoke. She straightened and looked at him. "I really do believe your daughter is more important than the roast."

"I agree. So it makes sense that you should be the one to check on her and see why she's upset. She's usually out for the count by this time in the evening."

There was nothing actually wrong with what he was saying, but once again Mollie was left with an increas-

ing sense of unease that none of her plans to get him to
spend more time with Jolene were working.

Later that night he was propped up in bed waiting for
her when she came out of the bathroom. "I was about
ready to come in there after you. What happened? Did
you fall asleep while you were soaking in the tub?" He
pushed the covers back on her side for her to crawl under them.

Absently she did so, saying, "I was thinking."

"About?"

"You."

"Boring subject."

"And why you refuse to have anything to do with
Jolene."

He reached over and turned off the light. "I don't
refuse. I just don't know anything about babies, that's
all."

"And you haven't tried to learn."

Silence greeted her remark.

She checked to make sure the baby monitor was on.
It was one of the first things she'd had installed after
they were married, explaining to Deke that she wanted
to be sure she could hear Jolene from this bedroom.

"Will you tell me why?" she finally asked.

After another weighty silence, he said in a very quiet
voice, "How I choose to behave around my child seems
to me to be my business. How much time I choose to
spend with her is also my business. Just because I married you does not give you any right to concern yourself in my business."

Mollie couldn't have been more shocked than if he'd slapped her. The phrase *"just because I married you"* seemed to echo in her ears.

Just because... the phrase seemed to grow louder and louder with each repetition. He'd made his reason for marrying her quite clear. It was very simple. He'd wanted someone to look after Jolene. That was it. There was no more to be said.

She was the one who had tried to make something more out of the arrangement. She'd wanted them to become a family...like Travis, Megan and Danny. She'd wanted—so much, so very much—and as the child she'd once been, she'd spun fantasies and dreams around the fact that she and Deke were now married and they were supposed to be living out their happily ever after.

She lay rigid on her side of the bed, hurting, but determined not to let on to Deke how much. Everything had worked out quite well for him, actually. Not only did he have a built-in baby-sitter, but he also had a cuddly playmate to keep him company in bed each night.

Mollie shot out of bed like a cannonball.

"Mollie? Where're you going?" he asked, reaching for the light. By the time he'd turned it on, she was already opening the door to the hallway. "What's wrong?"

She looked around at him. She felt as if something squeezed her heart, seeing him lying there, looking at her with a quizzical expression.

Of course he was confused. Hadn't she fallen into his arms like a ripe peach the first chance she got? He certainly didn't have to work at seducing her. She'd come to his bed more than ready, actually eager to experience all that they could share.

And they had shared so much. Even now, finally recognizing the futility of all her daydreams, she couldn't forget all that he had taught her, about herself and her own sexuality, as well as how to please him.

He sat up and swung his legs over the side of the bed. That's when she realized he was nude. He'd been waiting for her, as he so often did, to come to their bed to make love. Her throat tightened. *I will not cry,* she sternly reminded herself. Lamplight was very flattering to Deke Crandall, burnishing his bronzed and muscular good looks, highlighting his blond hair.

And she was a fool. An absolute fool.

"I, uh, I'm a little worried about Jolene," she stammered out. "I think I'll sleep closer to her tonight, in case she needs me."

His eyes narrowed. "But you can hear her on the monitor if she stirs at all. Wasn't that the whole point of having it installed?"

"I don't want to take the chance." She looked away, not wanting to see the look in his eyes. "It's much easier to be right next door to her. I'll see you in the morning. Good night." She was already closing the door when the sound of his voice stopped her.

"Mollie?"

"Yes?"

"Is this some kind of punishment because I won't talk to you about every blessed thing you want to know about me?"

"Punishment?"

He ran his hand through his hair and gave a disgusted sigh. "Withholding her favors was one of Patsy's favorite pastimes. Somehow I didn't figure you the type to play those kinds of games."

Mollie wrapped her arms around her waist, glad to be wearing her flannel nightgown that covered her from chin to toes. She forced herself to take a long, hard look at Deke. "You're absolutely right," she finally said. "I don't play games. Good night, Deke," she said, stepping into the hallway and closing the door behind her.

She was shaking so hard her teeth were chattering but somehow she managed to convince herself she'd gotten chilled from standing there in the cool hallway for so long after her hot bath.

It was true that she was concerned about Jolene. She was running a slight fever. The doctor said it wasn't all that unusual, but if it persisted to bring her in and he'd make sure she wasn't harboring an infection.

Concentrate on Jolene, she reminded herself, tiptoeing into the baby's room. Mollie knew that she was no match for Deke. He had years of experience on her that she would probably never have, regardless of the difference in their ages. Besides, he knew how to have a relationship. She, on the other hand, had never been involved with another man and had nothing to compare.

She was only now beginning to understand just how unhappy his marriage with Patsy had been. Some of his remarks sounded so cynical to her. And yet, he'd been so upset when Patsy had died that Mollie had assumed he was overcome with grief because his heart was broken. Even if that hadn't been the case...even if they hadn't been getting along, it made sense that he hadn't wanted her to die.

Mollie leaned over the railing of the crib and carefully smoothed Jolene's hair back from her cheek. She seemed to be resting well enough, thank God. It was amazing how the older Jolene became, the more she looked like Deke. They had the same hairline and the same eye color and shape.

Jolene also had a tiny dimple that flashed in her cheek when she smiled. Mollie had noticed it for the first time just last week. Deke had one, too, which only showed up when he grinned a certain, mischievous way.

After making sure that all the doors between their two rooms were open, Mollie crawled between the cold sheets of the spare bedroom.

Brrrr.

She'd forgotten after only a few weeks what it was like to sleep alone. How could she have so quickly succumbed to living and sleeping with Deke? She was such a fool, living in her own little world, believing that everything would turn out all right because that's the way she had everything planned.

Mollie forced herself to go to sleep, knowing that she had to make some changes in her life, starting tomorrow.

Remember, Jolene is the important one here. At least you can take care of yourself, she grimly pointed out to herself. At the moment, however, she wasn't feeling much more capable than Jolene. There was a deep, aching hole in her chest that she wasn't certain could ever be mended, but she had to try.

At least she'd had experience dealing with the grief of a lost loved one. The experience didn't make it any easier to face; it just assured her that she could get through this loss, too.

"Say, boss, I noticed one of the fence lines is down over in the back section," Deke's foreman mentioned the next morning. "You want me to send someone out there to restring it?"

"Let me go take a look. We may have to replace all the fences in that section. Good thing you noticed it. It will be easier to repair if we catch it before it gets any worse."

The back section was the toughest one to reach on the ranch since there was no road back in there. Deke saddled up one of his horses and rode out that way, knowing he would be gone for several hours. It was just as well. He had several things to think over. A day alone helped him do that.

Mollie was at the top of his list.

Damn, but she was stubborn. He'd learned that about her first off, of course, and had never been given a reason to change his mind about her since.

Take this morning, as an example. By the time he woke up, he could already smell the savory scent of bacon frying and the mouth-watering aroma of coffee brewing.

He'd slept like hell, twisting and turning, reaching out to the empty space beside him all night. What the devil had been wrong with her, that she'd suddenly got some burr under her saddle about sleeping in the other room?

Okay, he obviously must have made her mad last night. Well, that was too damn bad. Why did she keep poking and prying into things that were none of her damn business, anyway?

He was taking care of Jolene, wasn't he? He made sure there were qualified people to look after her. She certainly didn't need him following her around.

He guessed he would just let Mollie stew over whatever it was that had her marching out of his bedroom. If she didn't want to sleep with him, that was fine and dandy with him. He'd spent most of his life sleeping alone, for that matter. Hell's fire, he'd done a lot of that while he was married to Patsy. Women! Who needed 'em?

His thoughts were a variation on that theme for the rest of the day.

Deke didn't bother to ride back to the house at lunchtime. Instead he spent the day reattaching the wire he'd found lying on the ground as a makeshift barrier until they could order some new supplies to bring out to this area. There were several rotted posts that also needed replacing.

After mending that part of the fence, he spent the rest of the day riding along the boundaries of the entire section, making note of the number of new posts they would need as well as the number of feet of wire required.

It was almost dark when Deke finally returned to the house, cold and hungry. He walked into the kitchen and was greeted by savory scents that made his mouth water.

Mollie glanced up from stirring something on the stove and gave him a cheerful smile as soon as he walked inside. "Hi. Your foreman told me where you were. You should have said something to me before you left. I could have packed a lunch for you."

He shrugged out of his coat. "No problem. I made it okay, but I sure am hungry now," he admitted, inhaling deeply. His stomach growled to punctuate his statement.

"Dinner's ready now if you're ready to eat."

He glanced down at his filthy clothes and made a face. "Let me get cleaned up a little, first. I'm too dirty to sit down at the table at the moment."

Deke made a beeline for his bathroom, peeling off his clothes and relaxing beneath the soothing spray. He wasted no time scrubbing and rinsing himself off, then hurriedly drying himself off.

He returned to the bedroom for clean clothes and was pulling on a pair of jeans when it occurred to him that something was different about the bedroom. He reached for one of his flannel shirts and thoughtfully fastened the buttons down his chest while he looked around the room, puzzled.

And then it hit him. He looked back into the closet and started cursing. He walked over to the chest and started pulling out drawers. Empty. Every one of them.

He sat down on the edge of the bed and jerked on his socks, then strode back into the kitchen without bothering with his boots or slippers.

"Did you lose something?" she asked when he walked in. "I heard you slamming drawers and doors in there."

He leaned his shoulder against the doorjamb and folded his arms across his chest. "What could I have possibly lost?" he asked. "Everything is always put away in exactly the same place."

She put the last serving bowl on the table before turning to look at him. "Do you have a problem with that? I thought that was part of my job, making certain you had clean clothes when you needed them."

"Your job?" he repeated slowly, his eyes narrowing.

"Well, whatever you want to call it."

"What I call it is...you are my wife, not an employee."

She turned away and started cleaning off the countertops. "Well, yes, that's true, technically speaking."

He dropped his arms and straightened. "Maybe you'd better explain 'technically' to me. I'm just a country boy, remember."

She spun around and glared at him. "Don't you dare patronize me, Deke Crandall. Don't you dare! I am keeping your home, I am providing you with meals and I am caring for your daughter. That's what you wanted and that is exactly what you are getting."

"And no more?" he added softly. "Is that what you're saying? Is that why you moved out of our bedroom?"

"Not *our* bedroom. *Your* bedroom. I have my own, thank you." She went over to the table and sat down. "Your dinner's getting cold."

"And we can't have that, can we? I might dock your pay, or even worse, fire you. Is that what you think?" He strode over to the table, jerked out his chair and sat down, glaring at her.

She held her napkin in a stranglehold in her lap for several long minutes before she quietly said, "I'll tell you what I think, Deke. I think I totally misjudged you. And the funny part is that I have no one but myself to blame.

"You see, when I was a little girl I idolized you. You were the hero of every story I ever read or movie I ever saw. You were the central figure of every childhood fantasy I made up. Why, I thought my heart had been broken forever when I heard that you had gotten married, because in that hidden place in my heart where I stored my most secret dreams and desires, I had hoped that someday, if I did everything right in my life, I would grow up to marry my prince. Only the prince didn't wait for me to grow up."

She stood and placed her napkin beside her plate. "Too bad that after all these years I was given my chance after all, only to find out the prince had never been a prince in the first place. He was actually a frog."

Mollie walked out of the room, leaving Deke sitting alone at the table, stunned.

Chapter Ten

Deke wiped the back of his gloved hand across his sweaty brow, then paused to look at his watch. He and his men had been working since early morning on one of the most hated jobs on any spread—digging post-holes and stringing new wire. It was now almost two o'clock. They'd been working steadily except for a short break to eat whatever they'd brought with them for lunch.

In fact, they'd been working on this project off and on for several weeks, soon after Mollie had moved out of his bed and pointed out his failings as Prince Charming.

That had been in January. Now it was mid-March. Spring was already showing up in patches of protected hillsides in the form of fresh green grass and colorful spring wildflowers.

Of course they might get some more cold weather before winter gave up for the year, but there were more warm days than cold. The worst of winter was over.

Not that he missed it. He still got plenty of frost whenever he walked into his house. Mollie was frigidly polite to him. She was careful to respond to anything he said to her, but she kept her distance and made sure that she and Jolene were around him as little as possible.

He'd thought at first that he would wait a few days for her to cool off before attempting to make amends. Not that he was exactly sure what he'd done wrong, but hell, he was willing to listen to a list of his shortcomings if she'd take the time to point them out. But she never gave him a chance to say anything about anything.

Whew! but that woman had a temper.

He grinned to himself, just thinking about her. As far as that went, he spent most of his time thinking about her.

He missed her. He missed the way she used to be with him. He missed looking into those beautiful eyes of hers, seeing the—all right, he'd admit it—the adoring expression in them. So what was wrong with enjoying having someone adore you? he'd like to know. The irony hadn't escaped him. He'd lived with Patsy for almost a year before he discovered that she had never loved him. He'd lived with Mollie only a few short weeks before he discovered that she'd been in love with him for years.

Too bad he'd only found out when she'd discovered he wasn't worth loving. He could have told her that years ago and saved her the trouble.

He'd managed to figure out on his own that it probably had been her love for him that had caused her to come pounding on his door, offering to help him out. But that wasn't all he'd worked out in his head these past several weeks. He understood her a lot better now that he'd had time to look at their relationship.

It had been her love for him that had caused her to decide to marry him.

It had been her love for him that had caused her to make love with him . . . beautiful, life-affirming love-making that still caused him to dream the most erotic dreams of his life and wake up trembling and sweating and hurting with need.

He wouldn't go so far as to call himself a frog, exactly, but he was definitely a fool. He had managed to tick her off royally and he didn't have a hope in hell of convincing her to give him another chance.

Once a fool, always a fool, he guessed.

"Hey, boss, can we call it a day? We've set the last of the posts in this section. We can string wire tomorrow, can't we?"

Deke nodded. "Yeah, good idea. Let's call it a day."

The men cheered and immediately gathered their tools together before returning to their horses. By the time they reached the ranch yard everyone was already looking forward to taking a half day off and enjoying their first cold beer.

Deke went into the house, expecting to find Mollie there as usual and was surprised to find the house empty. He looked around. There was no note on the table, but then, she wouldn't have expected him back this early, either. Maybe she'd gone over to see Megan. On a hunch, he picked up the wall phone in the kitchen and called the O'Brien ranch. After several rings, Megan answered.

"Hi, Megan, is Mollie over there?"

"Oh, hi, Deke. She and Jolene were here this morning, but she had to leave for her doctor's appointment about one o'clock. She should be home shortly."

"Oh," he said blankly. "Yeah . . . guess I forgot."

Megan laughed. "Mollie said it was just a formality, seeing the doctor and all. You guys have known for weeks about the baby. Guess you're excited, huh?"

Deke's knees gave way and he sank to the floor. "Uh, yeah, that's about right," he managed to say. "I'll talk to you later, Megan . . . thanks," he offered as an afterthought before he hung up.

He pushed himself up off the floor and walked across to the refrigerator on wobbly legs. He found a bottle of beer and made his careful way over to the table to sit down.

Mollie was pregnant? And she'd known for weeks? She'd told Megan . . . and who else? Everyone but him? Mollie was going to have his baby?

Oh dear God . . . no.

Deke was still sitting at the table some time later when Mollie walked in with Jolene riding on her hip. "Oh, hi. You're home early. Did you get your refencing done?"

"Nope. Just decided to quit early." He waited but she didn't say anything more. Instead she began to talk in some indecipherable language to Jolene, removing her hat and coat and placing her in her high chair. Jolene babbled back, chuckling and banging on the tray in front of her to punctuate her remarks.

"So—" he finally said when she continued to bustle around the kitchen opening cabinets, going to the pantry, the refrigerator, the freezer "—where've you been?"

"Over at Megan's," she said without pausing or looking around at him. "Jolene and Danny are learning to play together really well. I think it's good for both of them to be around children near their own age."

"You were there all day?"

She paused in the act of pulling a mixing bowl out of the cabinet. "Most of it, yeah. I had a few errands to run."

He continued to sit there and watch her as she rapidly pulled a meal together. Finally she glanced around. "Aren't you going to shower before dinner?"

He looked down at his dirty clothes, only now aware that he had been sitting there for hours without a thought other than Megan's news. He pulled himself out of the chair. "Guess so."

"Deke?"

He paused in the doorway and looked around at her. "Yeah?"

"Is there something wrong? Did you get hurt today?"

He studied her for a long moment before he said, "Yeah, in a manner of speaking, but I'll probably recover."

"Do you need any help with bandages?"

He just shook his head and walked away.

Deke stood under the hottest water he could stand, trying to come to terms with what he'd learned. He'd never been so frightened in all his life when he'd heard that Mollie was pregnant.

Dear God, not Mollie, too! I can't lose Mollie. Even if she hates me, even if she'll never let me near her again, I can't lose her, too. Don't you understand? I love her! Maybe it was me that didn't understand, because what she makes me feel is so different from anything I've ever felt before. I know the doctor said that what happened to Patsy was a freakish thing, but that doesn't mean it couldn't happen to Mollie, too. I felt so bad losing Patsy because of the guilt for not loving her. Please don't take Mollie away from me as punishment. I'll do whatever I can. Will you please help me, God?

Mollie was feeding Jolene when he returned to the kitchen. She glanced up, looking a little harassed. "I'm sorry. I try to have her fed and in bed before you get home, but I guess the time slipped away from me today and then you came home early and—"

"It doesn't matter. I'm not that hungry, anyway."

He sat back down and watched Mollie feeding Jolene. The baby was almost a year old now. She was beginning to look like a person to him now, not a faceless little blob of humanity.

Jolene giggled, flashing two teeth in her bottom jaw, as well as a dimple in her cheek. Deke froze, suddenly intent on the baby's face. He studied her hair, her eyes, the shape of her brow, and watched for that betraying dimple. There! He saw it again.

Jolene didn't look anything like Patsy, he realized. Instead she was beginning to look more and more like...his mother. Her hair had grown quite a bit in the past few months, but it was still as light as it had been when she was born.

His mother had been a natural blonde, as well.

Deke felt as though he'd gotten a one-two punch to the gut today. He was still reeling.

"Upsy daisy, sweetie," Mollie said to Jolene. "Let's get you cleaned up and ready for bed...yes, I know you're tired. You've been such a good girl today. Let's get you a bath and then it's beddy-bye time." She lifted Jolene to her hip. "Dinner's almost ready, Deke. Why don't you go ahead and dish up something?"

"That's okay. I can wait for you."

"I'm going to be a while. She enjoys her bath and I usually let her play for a while."

"It's okay."

She shrugged. "Well, if you get tired of waiting, it's all there on the stove."

What had he done to himself with his stiff-necked pride? He'd deliberately denied himself the first year of his daughter's life. He'd made no effort to get to know her or to let her get to know him. Who had he thought he was punishing? Patsy? Himself?

When he heard the sound of laughter and water splashing down the hall Deke followed the sounds and ended up in the doorway of the bathroom watching his daughter destroy the entire area with unabashed glee.

After a particularly big splash she glanced up at him and broke into a toothy grin. "Dada! Dada-dada-da-da." She bounced and splashed both hands into the water.

Mollie glanced around in surprise, then smiled at Jo-lene. "Yes, honey, that's your daddy, come to see what a big mess you can make," she said casually. "Now, then, don't you think it's time you get out? I'll let you play an extra long time tomorrow, but I think that's enough for today. You've worn me out and I—"

"Why don't you let me take over?" he blurted out, surprising himself and Mollie. "I mean, at least let me dry her. Do you have her nightclothes laid out?"

"Uh, yes. They're lying on the dressing table." She lifted the dripping little girl out of the tub and wrapped her in a towel. "Are you sure you want to do this?"

"Oh, yeah. I'll probably make a mess of it, but I definitely want to try."

She sighed. "Thanks. I think I tried to cram too much into my day today. I'm beat." She handed him the squirming baby, saying, "Go to your daddy, honey."

Just like that he had his daughter in his arms for the first time.

She was a solid little bundle, and Deke could understand why Mollie could be exhausted from hauling her around. Was it good for her in her condition? Oh God. He didn't know. He didn't know and what if it wasn't? What could he do to help?

Jolene quickly demanded his entire attention as he attempted to dry her, powder her and place a diaper on her. The baby was in constant motion. She never once paused. The diaper was hanging around one leg when Mollie walked in. "Well, at least the bathroom's cleaned up a little. Here, let me help." She quickly flipped the baby back down and anchored both sides of the diaper, before sitting her up once more and dropping her nightgown over her head.

Deke was amazed at Mollie's dexterity. She was a natural at dealing with a perpetual-motion machine that pretended to be a baby. She lay her down into the crib and patted her back until Jolene's eyelids fluttered closed for the last time.

Deke took Mollie's hand and led her back into the kitchen. "Why don't you sit down and I'll fix both our plates. No reason to put everything out on the table tonight."

He knew it was a measure of how she must be feeling that she didn't argue with him. Instead she sank into her chair with a sigh. "Everything's probably cold by now."

"No. It's just fine. You really amaze me, the way you can put together a delicious meal in such a short time. That's a real talent you have."

She yawned. "Not really. It's just something I've done all my life. It comes second nature to me."

He waited until they finished eating, then suggested she get ready for bed while he cleaned up the kitchen. Once again she docilely followed his suggestion. This was not the Mollie he knew, fierce and independent, and he was becoming more and more concerned.

After everything was in its place in the kitchen, Deke went looking for Mollie and discovered her in bed fast asleep. She looked pale to him, and there were dark shadows beneath her eyes. God, he was such a jerk. She'd been pushing herself for weeks. He remembered Patsy's first few weeks. She'd been so sick. How had Mollie kept her condition from him? Things were beginning to make a little more sense to him now. That was why she spent so little time around him.

She was always up before he was, and then he was gone all day. He seldom came in for lunch. Perhaps she'd been able to nap when Jolene was down. He hoped so.

Thank God she'd decided to go to a doctor. He'd probably put her on the necessary vitamins and minerals.

Deke lost track of time as he stood there watching her sleeping. Then he made his decision.

Taking care not to awaken her, he scooped Mollie up into his arms and carried her down the hallway to his bedroom. He flipped the covers back with one hand before he gently lowered her to the bed, then stripped out of his clothes and crawled in beside her.

She didn't stir. He reached over and turned out the lamp, then gathered her into his arms. He had so much he needed to say to her. And he didn't want her out of his arms until he could tell her what was in his heart.

Mollie was having the most wonderful dream. She and Deke were somewhere; she wasn't sure where they were. There was a white sandy beach, a deeply blue lagoon, palm trees, tantalizing music... and Deke was holding her in his arms.

She ran her hand down his chest, feeling the muscles ripple and move beneath her fingers. Her hand continued to drift downward until she discovered his wonderfully aroused condition.

She moaned—or was it he who moaned?—as her fingers brushed across him, outlining and caressing him.

Then he was kissing her—hot, passionate kisses that made her shiver with need. He was touching her, finding her warm and ready and—

Mollie's eyes flew open. This was no dream! Deke was in bed with her and he was... Oh, my, yes, he certainly was...she clutched him to her, holding him tightly as he carefully moved over her, joining them once again.

Oh, yes, this was what she had been missing for so long. She'd spent so many sleepless nights thinking about holding him and loving him and now...and now...it was real.

She was quickly propelled into a fierce release, sobbing into his shoulder as he followed her lead. He rolled, still holding her tightly against him, until she was lying on top of him, draped across his relaxed body. Only then did Mollie realize they were in his bed.

"How did I get in here?" she asked sometime later when she could gather enough energy to inquire.

"I kidnapped you, I'm afraid. You're probably never going to believe that I didn't intend for us to make love when I brought you in here. That wasn't the plan I had in mind, anyway. But when I woke up and found your hand wrapped around me like that, I'm afraid I lost whatever control I thought I had."

She smiled, her head resting on his shoulder. "I thought I was dreaming."

"I *knew* I was."

They broke into soft, shared laughter before they settled into a companionable silence once again.

"Mollie, there's something I need to tell you."

"Now?" she drowsily protested.

"Not necessarily now, but that was my reason for bringing you in here. I don't want you out of my sight until we've had a chance to talk, okay?"

"I'm not going anywhere," she murmured before she gave a little wriggle and settled herself more comfortably on top of him. He smiled with relief and a heart full of love, wrapped his arms around her and fell back asleep.

Everything else could wait, as long as Mollie was in his arms where she belonged.

"You thought what?"

Mollie was sitting in the middle of his bed, hugging a pillow to her middle and staring at him in disbelief.

Although it was morning, neither one of them had given a thought to getting out of bed. Thankfully Jolene had taken her early-morning bottle and gone back to sleep.

Deke had been trying his best to explain, but he was obviously not doing a very good job. "I know. I know it sounds like I'm making all of this up, but you need to understand about Patsy and me."

"Yes. I guess I do."

"After the first year of our marriage, she admitted to me that she'd married me on the rebound. That she was really in love with somebody else. A guy who had dumped her. He'd never been the most stable character and she was tired of trusting the wrong kinds of guys. She figured I was different. I owned this property. I was alone and lonely. She convinced both of us that she was madly in love with me. So we got married. I think she really did try, but she was bored here.

"After telling me the truth she left and was gone for several weeks. Then she came back and said she wanted to make our marriage work. That's the way our relationship was for years. The last time, she'd been gone for six months before she came back and I thought she was gone for good. In a way, I was glad. I was tired of the emotional turmoil, tired of trying to be what she wanted when even she wasn't sure what it was she wanted.

"Then she suddenly showed up one day, saying she'd finally gotten all of that out of her system. She said she wanted to settle down and raise a family. I told her I didn't want a family. That things were too rocky between us and that I wasn't sure I wanted to even make the effort anymore. I wouldn't even touch her again until she convinced me she was on the pill. Even then, I did my best to ignore her."

He sighed, scratching his jaw. "Then one night she caught me in a weak moment and seduced me. I know that sounds like a dumb way to put it—"

"Not really. I find you very seducible, myself. I can understand her reasoning perfectly well."

"Well, anyway, soon after that, almost too soon I always thought, she admitted to me that she had lied about being on the pill because she'd wanted to get pregnant. And she was. So what was I supposed to think?"

"That she was pregnant, perhaps?" she teased.

"Well, yes, I believed that part of it, all right, but I also believed that the only reason she'd bothered to come back to me was because she'd gotten herself pregnant and needed to make me think it was mine."

"So you're sitting there—lying there—actually telling me that all this time you've never believed that Jolene was yours? Deke Crandall, that has absolutely got to be the dumbest thing I've ever heard. All you have to do is look at Jolene to see that she looks just like you!''

"Like my mother." He gently corrected her. "Yeah, I know that now. But the thing is, I had never really looked at her before. To see her, I mean. Until yesterday. I was watching you feed her and noticing how much she's changing. And that's when I saw— That's when I realized that— Aw, hell. What can I say? I've been a complete idiot.''

"Well, I guess that explains why you haven't had anything to do with her all this time. You've been thinking that you were raising Patsy's child by some unknown guy. I guess that would be a little hard for any man to take.''

"No. It was stupid. Jolene was an innocent baby who had lost her mother and needed at least one parent. I was too stiff-necked to see that before yesterday. But don't worry, I've paid for my attitude. I've missed out on all these months, almost a year, of her life. What I needed a long time ago was a good, swift kick in the rear.''

"That thought had occurred to me on more than one occasion, I must admit.''

He grabbed her pillow away from her and pulled her back down to him. "C'mere, you. I don't like having you so far away.''

She allowed him access to her body but her mind was still racing with his confession. "So. Even though you didn't think Jolene was your daughter, you weren't going to tell anybody. You were just going to raise her like she was yours.''

''Well, of course. What else could I do?''

She grinned. ''Knowing you, probably nothing.''

He eyed her uncertainly. ''So. What do you think? Am I still a frog?''

''*We-ellll*, maybe not.''

''Could I work on becoming a prince-in-training?''

''If I hadn't been so mad, I would have never told you about all that. I am so embarrassed. The idea of telling you of all people!''

''I'm glad you did. I just wish I'd known you back then when you were growing up, your eyes filled with starry visions and dreams. If only I'd been aware of you, I know I would have waited for you to grow up.''

''But then you wouldn't have had Jolene.''

When he didn't say anything, she said, ''I know she's going to be a touchy subject for you.''

''It's not that. I was thinking about how angry I was with Patsy during her pregnancy, then how guilty I was when she died. I kept thinking that maybe it was my fault. If I hadn't been so cold and distant with her maybe she would have lived ... If I'd done something different, she would have been different.''

''Well, I have to say that you have cold and distant down to an exact science.''

''You're not exactly a heat wave, yourself, you know. Has anybody ever discussed your temper with you?''

''Me? Temper? I don't have a temper.''

"I stand corrected." He eyed her for a long moment. "What do I have to do or say to get you to move back into my bed permanently?"

"What would you like to do or say?"

"Well, I'd like to tell you how much I love you, and how much I've missed having you in my bed, and how touched I am by your devotion to my daughter, and how I've been waiting ever so patiently for you to break the news to me that you're having my baby, and how—"

"What? What did you say?" She slid off him and started hitting him with a pillow. "How did you know? How could you possibly have figured out that I—"

"Megan told me."

She stared at him in horror. "Megan told you! When?"

"Yesterday when I called to see if you might be over there. She spoke as though I already knew and I didn't want to make her feel like she'd said something she shouldn't have. So when did you intend to tell me?"

"Oh, Deke," she whispered. "I didn't mean for you to find out that way. I'm so sorry."

He stared into her eyes for a long time before he replied. "Yeah. Me, too."

"I wanted to move back in here the very first night but I was hurting so badly, and I needed some space. Then after I realized that I might be pregnant, I didn't want to move in just because I was going to have your baby. You probably don't believe me, but I had intended to tell you just as soon as the doctor confirmed it. I knew that we were going to have to talk about what was going on with us, and I was scared. We'd never discussed having a family of our own. I was afraid you were going to be so angry and yet, I certainly had some help in getting into this interesting position." She paused, watching him closely. "Did you really mean it?"

"Mean what? That I want you to move back in here? You're damn right, I mean it."

"No. Did you really mean it when you said you love me? You don't have to pretend, you know, just because of the baby. It's okay with me if you just like me at first. I can handle that until we've had more time together, and learned to get along better."

"Come here, you," he said, pulling her back into his arms. "It's okay if I like you?" he repeated in a falsetto. "How kind, how noble you are, Mrs. Crandall. A regular saint, I must say. Well, I'm telling you right here and now that I want a lot more than that from you, don't kid yourself. And I intend to spend each and every day of the rest of my life showing you exactly how much I love you."

She sighed with unfeigned pleasure, allowing him to cuddle her against him. "I'm finding it all a little hard to believe. I guess I was hoping that eventually you'd want to make love to me again, but other than that—"

"Eventually? I've wanted you every single night since you moved into the other room, but I wasn't going to beg. If you didn't want to sleep with me, I was trying my best to behave like a gentleman and accept your decision.''

''Could it be possible that we both have rather strong tempers?''

''And that we are both rather stubborn?''

She laughed. ''Oh, our poor baby. He'll be quite a handful.''

''He?''

''Well, that's what I'm hoping for, anyway. Don't you think Jolene needs a little brother?''

''I think Jolene is luckier than she'll ever know. Thank God Mollie O'Brien came marching into our lives, a crusading spirit determined to teach us both more about love, loving and being loved.''

''And have I?''

''Oh, yes, ma'am. More than I can ever show you. But that doesn't mean I'm not going to keep trying,'' he replied, his hands roaming over her body and causing her to quiver.

She kissed him while she did some exploring of her own. When she finally pulled away to catch her breath, she gave him a beatific smile. ''Then I guess I've accomplished my mission, after all.''

Epilogue

"Mollie? Are you in here? I can't find you for all these flower arrangements!"

Megan came bouncing into the hospital room, grinning from ear to ear. "What did Deke do? Buy out the entire supply at the florists?"

"Of course not. These are from friends, members of the church and that one over there has your and Travis's names on it." She grinned. "You see? Chad and I are very popular these days."

"I don't know how to break the news to you, honey, but you're playing a poor second these days. Deke's been pointing out Chad to everybody who passes by the nursery window, handing out cigars, looking like he personally delivered him."

"Oh, Megan, you should have seen him at the delivery. He was so sweet, trying to hide how uptight he was. You know how worried he's been ever since he found out I was pregnant. He tried hard to hide it, but it was always there. And yet he insisted on being with me through all the stages, including delivery. The doctor had to take him aside and convince him that I was doing fine, the baby was doing fine and that there hadn't been any complications."

"I know. He's been talking to Travis about his feelings these past few months. I think it's been good for both of them. They've grown quite close to each other." She patted her protruding tummy. "I just hope they haven't decided to go into some kind of competition here. I swear, ever since Chad was born Travis is acting like he thinks we're behind in this baby business, with you already having two."

"Speaking of babies, who's watching Danny and Jolene?"

"Maribeth. She said she'd come up tonight and see you. Another week and she would have been back at College Station."

"She seems to be enjoying college."

"Yes, thank God. She's really eager to finish up so she can get her degree."

"I can always go back and get mine if I want to. Deke has already mentioned it more than once."

"But you hated college, didn't you?"

"Yeah, to be honest with you, I really did."

"I'm sorry I kept pushing you into doing something you didn't want to do. I hope I don't make the same mistake with Maribeth."

"She'll stand up to you."

"Just like you did."

"Yeah."

They smiled at each other in complete understanding and harmony.

Once again the door to Mollie's hospital room opened. This time, Travis walked in, holding a cigar. "I swear, woman, that kid of yours got here more than half growed. He's huge. Figure he'll be walking out of here on his own steam?"

"I wouldn't put it past him. He's already letting everybody around the place know whenever he's hungry. I've been used to a dainty little girl. Chad's going to whip us all into shape."

While they were chatting, Megan had been wandering around the room, reading the cards on all the flower arrangements. She paused in front of a planter in the shape of a frog with a large knapsack on his back. He sat with long, bony legs dangling over the side, crossed at the ankles. He wore a golden crown cocked over one eye, while the other eye was closed in a wink. He wore a very smug-looking smile on his face.

"This one doesn't have a card," she said pointedly.

Mollie grinned. "It didn't need one."

"Who's it from?"

"Deke. It's kind of a private joke between us."

"Ah. As in kiss the toad and he becomes a prince?"

Mollie laughed. "Close enough."

"Well. I'm glad that Deke has turned out to be such a wonderful husband for you. He looks years younger than he did last winter. You must be good for him."

"He's been good for me, too."

"And he's so good with Jolene. I offered to keep her at our place while you were here, but he said he didn't mind looking after her. He wasn't going to get anything done around the ranch until he had you back home, anyway."

"Well, at least I had enough warning to get her over to you before I had to come to the hospital. I don't think he could have been at both places at once."

"Knowing Deke, he'd try. I wonder if he'll ignore Chad his first year like he did Jolene? You know, some men are really uncomfortable around babies. Maybe Deke's one of them."

"Somehow I doubt it. He just had some healing to do, first. I get the feeling he's looking forward to learning how to care for a newborn."

Deke peeked around the door. "Hi. Thought I'd let you know I'm leaving. I need to pick up Jolene and give Maribeth a rest."

Travis took Megan by the arm. "Hey, we'll get on out of here and give you a minute alone with your wife." He rubbed his hand across Megan's stomach. "If this keeps up, the family's going to have to add a larger maternity wing to the hospital."

Deke walked over and leaned over the bed, kissing Mollie. "I don't think we need any more, do you, honey?" He smiled at the other couple. "I'm too old for all this. I think I'll leave the bigger families to you young people," he said, causing them all to burst into laughter. He looked at the others. "What? What was so funny about that?"

Travis thumped him on the shoulder. "The idea that you're too old for anything...right, Mollie?" he asked, disappearing through the door with Megan before Mollie could think of a reply.

"What was that all about, anyway?" Deke asked his smiling wife.

"Just my crazy family. You should be used to them by now."

"I'm getting better, I think. I never had much of a family before. Being around the O'Brien clan has been a whole new experience for me."

"Do you mind becoming an honorary member of the clan?"

He leaned over once again and kissed her, slowly, with a great deal of feeling. "I wouldn't have missed it for the world."

*   *   *   *   *

DAUGHTERS OF TEXAS *continues with*
Maribeth O'Brien's romance.
THE GROOM I PRESUME?—Don't miss it!
Coming to you from Silhouette Desire—as part
of the exciting Celebration 1000! Party!

COMING NEXT MONTH

#1144 MOST WANTED DAD—Arlene James
Fabulous Fathers/This Side of Heaven
Amy Slater knew the teenage girl next door needed a sympathetic ear—as did her father, Evans Kincaid. But Amy found it hard to be just a *friend* to the sexy lawman, even though she'd sworn never to love again....

#1145 DO YOU TAKE THIS CHILD?—Marie Ferrarella
The Baby of the Month Club
One night of passion with handsome Slade Garret left Dr. Sheila Pollack expecting nothing...except a baby! When Slade returned and demanded marriage, Sheila tried to resist. But Slade caught her at a weak moment—while she was in labor!

#1146 REILLY'S BRIDE—Patricia Thayer
Women were in demand in Lost Hope, Wyoming, so why did Jenny Murdock want stubborn rancher Luke Reilly, the only man *not* looking for a wife? Now Jenny had to convince Reilly he needed a bride....

#1147 MOM IN THE MAKING—Carla Cassidy
The Baker Brood
Bonnie Baker was in Casey's Corners to hide from love, not to be swept away by town catch Russ Blackburn! Gorgeous, devilish Russ got under her skin all right...but could Bonnie ever risk love again?

#1148 HER VERY OWN HUSBAND—Lauryn Chandler
Rose Honeycutt had just blown out her birthday candles when a handsome drifter showed up on her doorstep. Cowboy Skye Hanks was everything she'd wished for, but would his mysterious past keep them from a future together?

#1149 WRANGLER'S WEDDING—Robin Nicholas
Rachel Callahan would do anything to keep custody of her daughter. So when Shane Purcell proposed a pretend engagement, Rachel decided to play along. Little did she know that the sexy rodeo rogue was playing for keeps!

MILLION DOLLAR SWEEPSTAKES

SWP-M96

As seen on TV!

Free Gift Offer

With a Free Gift proof-of-purchase from any Silhouette® book,
you can receive a beautiful cubic zirconia pendant.

This gorgeous marquise-shaped stone is a genuine cubic
zirconia—accented by an 18" gold tone necklace.

(Approximate retail value $19.95)

Send for yours today…

compliments of *Silhouette*®

To receive your free gift, a cubic zirconia pendant, send us one original proof-of-purchase, photocopies not accepted, from the back of any Silhouette Romance™, Silhouette Desire®, Silhouette Special Edition®, Silhouette Intimate Moments® or Silhouette Shadows™ title available in February, March or April at your favorite retail outlet, together with the Free Gift Certificate, plus a check or money order for $1.75 U.S./$2.25 CAN. (do not send cash) to cover postage and handling, payable to Silhouette Free Gift Offer. We will send you the specified gift. Allow 6 to 8 weeks for delivery. Offer good until April 30, 1996 or while quantities last. Offer valid in the U.S. and Canada only.

Free Gift Certificate

Name: _____

Address: _____

City: _____ State/Province: _____ Zip/Postal Code: _____

Mail this certificate, one proof-of-purchase and a check or money order for postage and handling to: SILHOUETTE FREE GIFT OFFER 1996. In the U.S.: 3010 Walden Avenue, P.O. Box 9057, Buffalo NY 14269-9057. In Canada: P.O. Box 622, Fort Erie,

---

FREE GIFT OFFER   079-KBZ-R

ONE PROOF-OF-PURCHASE

To collect your fabulous FREE GIFT, a cubic zirconia pendant, you must include this original proof-of-purchase for each gift with the properly completed Free Gift Certificate.

079-KBZ-R

You're About to Become a *Privileged Woman*

Reap the rewards of fabulous free gifts and benefits with proofs-of-purchase from Silhouette and Harlequin books

Pages & Privileges™

It's our way of thanking you for buying our books at your favorite retail stores.

PROOF OF PURCHASE
SR-PP114
Offer expires October 31, 1996

**Harlequin and Silhouette—
the most privileged readers in the world!**

For more information about Harlequin and Silhouette's PAGES & PRIVILEGES program call the Pages & Privileges Benefits Desk: 1-503-794-2499

SR-PP114